TRAPPED
An Anthology of Horror Stories

I0551890

Edited by Dorothy Davies

TRAPPED
An Anthology of Horror Stories

GRAVESTONE PRESS

CONTENTS

CONTENTS

Code for Life

Michael B Fletcher

I was on my stomach, the floor hard stone. The air was soft and warm, no strong odours, no discernible scents. A vague breeze rustled quietly.

I lifted my head with difficulty to look in the direction I was pointing. A corridor led into the distance: light and dark; light and dark merging so far ahead I had difficulty focussing.

I attempted to roll over but something held me down. I struggled fruitlessly until I realised that a neck collar fixed me securely to the surface, one arm free, the other held by an armlet shackled into the stone floor in front of me. My yells echoed, giving me the feeling of emptiness in a vast space, until I had the ominous thought that I might attract the attention of something undesirable. I stopped yelling.

What was happening?

Last thing I recalled was walking in the town late at night, thinking I was ready for my hotel bed. I had been to the mathematics conference and then to the supper. I had endured the small talk of a number of people, most talking through their heads about formulae and numbers they had no real concept of. For the most part I had kept quiet, nodded at the appropriate time and not locked horns with any of the idiots there.

7

There were few I regarded as my intellectual equal and fortunately I was astute enough not to let them know what I thought. That is until Finlayson began to pontificate.

I'd known him in the department for a number of years and fortunately our paths seldom crossed. He was one of those individuals you instinctively disliked. Nose slightly in the air, always ready with a comment and making sure he knew the right people. Yes, someone to avoid.

But, blame it on the particularly strong local drink, the Milk of Lions. Seemed innocuous enough but packed a punch and there was plenty on hand. I had one or two more than I should have, which lowered my natural caution. It made me counter Finlayson's latest formula, something about the secure use of numbers in a way that was almost impossible to decode. I ridiculed his idea and didn't notice when he showed his anger at my over-riding of his comments. Even when he slipped away I rattled on, confident in my argument and emboldened by the drink.

Outside, the air made me regret I had drunk so much and I looked forward to sleep.

I listened for a sound, any sound to give me a clue of where I was. The corridor looked well-used, old but the light and dark sections made me think it was daylight, sun and shade. I struggled again, but to no avail, so I slumped back to the floor.

The scrape of a shoe behind me broke the silence, but I couldn't see who it was. A searing

8

pain hit my side and I screamed, the echoes blasting the empty space. Again! The pain was white-hot.

'Stop!'

'Mr High And Mighty!' a recognisable voice hissed. 'Not so cock-sure now, eh?'

'Finlayson?'

'Doctor Finlayson to you.'

'Why are you doing this? Let me loose.'

'No, because you deserve to be.'

'Why?'

'No-one, but no-one, ridicules me. Superior intellect, hah.'

'Let me go. Please!'

'Please, now? Last night you were so sure of yourself, your superior knowledge of mathematics. Too smart for the rest of us.'

'What do you want?'

'What I want is for you to pit your wits against me. Use your so-called abilities to solve a small puzzle. Set by me, your intellectual inferior. If you solve it you will be freed. If you fail, well, no-one will find you. Few people come here but someone will, in a month or so. Too late for you, though.'

'You can't do this. I'll be missed. They'll come looking.' I wriggled against my bonds, trying to get a glimpse of my tormenter, but all I could see was a black boot ready to deliver another blow.

'Ahh!'

'Listen, oh fabulous mathematician. You can free yourself. After all, you have the means and the clues lie ahead of you.'

'What?'

'I'm going. Another lecture on. One that I, in my meagre capacity, am to deliver.'

I heard the scuff of his boots as he turned away.

'Wait. What clues? What do I have to do?'

'Very simple. Enter the correct numbers into the armlet and your bonds will release. Fail and the band will tighten.'

'Tighten? What numbers? What do you mean?'

'Ah, it lies ahead of you. Goodbye.'

'Wait!' I yelled as the sound of his footsteps faded away.

I banged my head on the stone in frustration.

My head throbbed and my throat dried up. *Was he serious? Did he mean me to lie here until I either solved the puzzle or died? What puzzle?*

'Finlayson!' I screamed to the silence. I craned a look down the long corridor. The light and dark was mesmerising. *Maybe he meant a combination of numbers such as my room number and hotel address. Yes.*

I tapped in room 327 and the street address of 304 Arcadian Way. The armlet screen glowed red: invalid password. A tingle throbbed in the collar banded around my neck. I tried again, reversing the numbers. Invalid password. And again the band tingled. I thought of entering the number of conference delegates. Again, invalid password. This time I thought I noticed a slight tightening of the band.

Why was Finlayson so smug? What mathematical problem could he think of to fool me? I went through numerous formulas and any potential mathematical combination I could think

10

of. Invalid password. All I achieved was more of a sore neck, the band tight around my throat.

I had a raging thirst, too. I noticed the light dying away. Night had come.

At some point I must have fallen asleep, exhausted. I awoke to silence, throat sore as hell and still shackled to the floor. The corridor ahead was its usual patterning of light and dark, no-one around and no clue how to break my bonds. I thought I'd kill Finlayson when I saw him as I lay there in a wallow of self-pity.

The patterning of light and dark struck a chord. It was the same as the day before. Same hues. *Could there be numbers there? After all, it lay ahead of me, if Finlayson's clue was to be believed.*

I tried several random series of numbers. Again, invalid password flashing in red. But this time additional words filled me with horror; system will lock after three more attempts.

'Bloody Finlayson!' I swore as the tight band around my throat only allowed me to yell. 'Helpppp!'

While I lay there trying not to think of my raging thirst and choking throat a startling revelation came. *What could he do that could outsmart me? Something about the place and the patterning, "ahead of me"? If he could think of it, then I could solve it.* I racked my brain trying to remember Finlayson's formula from the lecture.

The solution became obvious, even showing a modicum of craftiness. I peered down the long corridor.

'Yes!' The light and dark portions were regular, having a pattern, one that came to me in a blinding flash. A bloody barcode; numbers in variations between the light and dark. I thought back to the mathematics, recalling that each number from zero to nine was represented by different light and dark segments in blocks of seven. *But what were they?*

'Fuck,' I breathed through my constricted airway, my body cramping as I lay there. Dying was a great incentive to solving the puzzle.

The light down the corridor gave the clues. I allowed my mathematical brain to work through the options.

'Ah!' I rasped. 'Five, three, seven.' I edged my free hand to the armlet and punched in the numbers.

Invalid password. Two entries remain.

'Christ!' The band around my neck tightened so I drew air in with difficulty.

Surely the patterns represent the numbers I'd punched in? Wait, I mustn't have seen the final number due to the unevenness of the stone floor.

I tried the new numbers, 'five, three, eight.'

The armlet screen flashed red. Invalid password. One entry remaining.

The band tightened further, pulling my head to the floor. *What mistake had I made? Why didn't it work? After all I was smarter than Finlayson. The idiot couldn't beat me.*

I peered down the corridor with difficulty. '*Shit!*' I thought, realising the light entering the corridor was changing, afternoon coming on making the barcodes harder to see, harder to decipher. I had little option but to go for it. *What had I done wrong?*

Then I saw it, another shadow making a number seem to be a three rather than a six, obvious when you looked at it. *Yes, that was it. They were the numbers to save my life and give me my freedom.*

I took a difficult breath and entered the numbers. Five, three, six.

I pressed the last number. A figure moved silently from the shadows at the end of the corridor. The patterns shifted with his movement. The last number changed.

The band tightened, cutting off my airway. Finlayson's laughter echoed down the corridor. I didn't need to see the words to know my fate.

Music Man

Mark Towse

Even I know he isn't quite in tune, but the old man with the discoloured beard sings as though his life depends on it. Eyes screwed tight shut, head bopping up and down, he taps his worn-out shoes against the pavement ahead.

"He's not going to do it," Harry blurts. "Nothing but fresh air between those legs."

"I am! I'm just waiting for the right time, okay?" The last word comes out as a croak.

"Or perhaps a vagina," Harry mumbles.

Dad always says never give in to peer pressure, but I'm not sure he ever experienced what's it like to be the new kid in school, sitting in a crowded and noisy dining hall, feeling like the loneliest person in the world.

"The man's blind, Tom," Sam says. "Look at the white cane. You could stand in front of him butt naked and gyrating, meat stick slapping against your thighs and he'd never know."

I turn my attention back to Yellow Beard, his matching fingers strumming at the old guitar. "What's the point then?"

"Because we're bored and it's your turn!" Harry spits impatiently. "But if you're too fucking chicken…"

My dad doesn't like Harry and neither do I, but beggars can't be choosers, as Mum would say. Sam took me under his wing which made his tag-along, Harry, all kinds of bitter.

"It doesn't feel right, though," I utter as the man launches into a new tune.

Too many times, I've walked this ashen plaaaaace

"For fuck's sake, Tom, it's just a coin!" Sam spits. "We're not asking you to kneel down and choke his rooster."

Dreaming of sand, the sun on my faaaaace

"He won't do it," Harry says.

But death hangs in the barren air

My skin prickles a warning as I snap my head from left to right. Some adults are wrapped up in awkward chit chat, others are stuffing their car with the week's groceries, but it suddenly seems much busier than before. This is pure wrong and I know it.

Carried on waves that haunt this lair

My heart pounds against my chest, building tension and importance. *Shit.* I watch the huddle of people through the entrance and as the doors slowly close behind them to the sound of the screaming guitar.

"Now!" Sam commands.

I unclench my hands and make my move towards the open case.

But I carry on down this rooooaaaaaad

The slap of my sneakers against the ground seems impossibly loud, but the guy is lost in his song and pays me no attention. I'm just another shopper, no change to spare, increasing their urgency on the way past.

Singing my worthless songs of madness

I glance over my shoulder, praying for a reason not to do it, I only see Sam and Harry looking my way, teeth gritted together and nodding in accidental synchronisation to the current guitar riff. Everyone else appears oblivious to the man's wailings.

Oh yeah, I'll carry on. I'll carry ooooon

I swoop down, my eyes drawn to the shiniest coin in the guitar case. But I can't get hold of it. Chewed nails down to the skin offer no leverage and all I'm doing is chasing it around the stiff purple velvet. The smell of stale tobacco permeates the air so strongly that it almost forces a cough.

Cuz hope is my melody, my way out of darkness

Someone else pulls into the car park. It has to be now. Finally, I pinch the coin a few inches above the case, fingers trembling, half-expecting it to fall or for a bony hand to clamp across my shoulder. But he's lost in a different world, putting on the performance of his life.

The slam of a car door prompts me into action and I snap my hand away and slide the coin into my pocket, screwing my face up as I make a run towards my new friends. I'm convinced someone saw the whole thing, expecting at any second to hear calls of "Thief!" but I'm almost home and dry. Ahead, Sam offers a thumbs up and Harry a scowl of disappointment.

Made it!

Although I can't contain the smile of relief, I hear my father's warnings of following the crowd. There's an accompanying twist in my gut and a sharp sting in my pocket adds further weight to his words.

"You're one of us now, Tom," Sam says, but his voice is distant, wrapped in layers of guilt and notes from that guitar that are suddenly so loud in my head.

"You okay, mate? You look a little shaky," Harry says, lips curled into his familiar sneer.

I offer a quick nod, but I don't feel okay. Not at all. The tarmac below no longer feels solid and the world is beginning to spin. Fast.

This is why I sing the bluuuuues

The man's voice carries a gravelly coarseness that reverberates painfully up and down my spine. An accompanying searing pain in my thigh continues to remind me of the coin's presence, but it's the least of my worries now.

"Tom!" Sam's tinny voice floats across over the impossibly loud guitar.

To see her face, I'll pay my duuuuues

Words rattle in my head until each one brands itself painfully into my brain. Chords screech, building towards an ear-bleeding crescendo.

Sam mouths my name, but I hear nothing above the man's gravelly and desolate voice.

The chances are slim; I can't denyyyyy

All I can hear and all I can think about are the words that fill my head. It's too much.

Still, there's nothing left to do but tryyyyy

Like a lonely groupie, I begin swaying back and forth.

Going to—

My eyes screwed tightly shut-in anticipation and I feel only slight discomfort on my back. I remain perfectly still, wary that perhaps I'm in shock and at any moment, nerve endings will begin to scream.

The music stops. Something else in the background, now. What is that? The ocean? Am I unconscious, dreaming perhaps? It would explain the lack of pain.

I open my eyes to no looming faces of concerns, something crunching beneath my palm. Dread consumes me.

This place is—ashen.

Tears come without warning, my head swamped with flashbacks of breakfast this morning—Mum ribbing Dad about putting empty cereal boxes back in the cupboard and not putting the lid back on the margarine.

This isn't a dream; it's because I took that goddamned coin!

Like a child, I drag my knees towards my chin, curling into a ball and wishing nothing more than to be back at the breakfast table. I take in my surroundings, rocking back and forth, feeling even lonelier than the kid in the dinner hall picking at his lunch. The sky is a montage of swirling grey and, on either side of me, waves of red curl on top of one another and crash back into the bubbling crimson sea with enormous ferocity. Ahead and behind is an endless landscape of black rock and ash.

And that smell.

"Hello," I croak.

Nothing.

I push myself up, dusting the blackness from my pants. "Hello."

One foot in front of the other, I tentatively head in the direction I'm facing, every so often glancing around at my blackened footprints, trying to ignore the lump in my throat and the now-familiar pressure behind my eyes.

So bleak.

"But I carry on down this road." My voice croaks with grief, but the distraction helps stem further tears. "Singing my worthless songs of madness."

I should have listened, shouldn't have caved to peer pressure.

"Oh, yeah, I'll carry on." *Dad.* "I'll carry on."

A solitary tear rolls down my right cheek.

"Cuz *hope is my melody, my way out of this darkness.*"

Heavy with hopelessness, my legs buckle in resignation, but I force myself onwards.

"This is why I sing the blues."

I didn't even say goodbye to Mum when I left the house this morning.

"To see her face, I'll pay my dues."

In the distance, I hear a guitar playing me into the next line.

"The chances are slim; I can't deny."

It's him, the Music Man! Each chord played exactly as I remember it, as though I could ever forget.

"Still, there's nothing left to do but try."

With each footstep, each word, the music draws closer until it abruptly stops and only the sounds of crashing waves remain. The man steps out from behind a black rock, one arm wrapped around the guitar, the other waving me towards him, as though he can—

"We see down here," he shouts. "Not that there's much to see; that's the cruelty of it."

"Am I dead?" I utter, not really wanting an answer.

"Not quite, but as good as, I suppose. Your heart still pumps, but he owns your soul now—bought it with that silver coin you plucked from my case."

"I want to go home." I won't cry again. I won't. "I didn't mean to take the coin; it was just a stupid bet."

The man nods. "I know, son, I know, but it's not as easy as that."

"Tell me what's happening," I croak. "Please!"

Music Man rests his guitar against the rock and lets out a sigh. "He loves his music; loves the blues. Been playing for him for nigh on five years and he still won't let me back, figures I've still got my best performance in me."

"I—I don't understand."

"Do you play guitar, kid? Sing?"

"No."

"Neither did I, but you will. If you're lucky, that is. He's looking for that one performance, you see—the perfect combination of lyrics and emotion—the one that brings him to his knees, makes him feel what it's like to be—human. If only

20

for a moment. Do that, and he'll send you back home. No catch."

"But you look like you're really trying, singing your heart out? And you say that you've been here—"

"Almost five years, yeah. I don't know what he's looking for, to tell you the truth, but he saw potential in me and I'll never stop trying. I want it for myself now, a slave to the music as much as to him."

"What if I won't? What if I can't?" My heart is racing, legs heavy with fear.

"The moment he suspects you stop playing for your life is when it all ends. Up there, your heart will stop and down here, your soul will be tossed into the Dead Sea and you'll burn for eternity and feel every minute of it." He tucks a finger into his threadbare scarf as though it's suddenly too tight. "Any more questions?"

My mind races, skin prickling with anxiety and fear. "How do we get up there?"

"He opens the door when it's time, but don't get too excited, kid. We don't get to play on home soil and he only lets us up there to remind us of what we're missing, giving us hope and the will to become better. Sometimes to recruit." The man takes a few steps towards the furious sea, tapping his fingers against his thigh. "As I said, we're blind up there, but it's better than nothing. The smell of a hot dog, the feel of the breeze on your face. Besides, he figures it makes us play better—forced to draw from memories and fewer distractions."

"But I told you; I can't play the guitar, can't sing."

"I can teach you all that down here. You just gotta hope he sees a spark in you."

The smell of death gets undoubtedly stronger. Waves begin to crash with further ferocity, small globs of fizzing violence landing only a few feet away from us. "He's coming," the man whispers, shifting from one foot to the next. "Just adrenaline, kid. You'll learn how to use the fear."

"What now?"

"Your first audition."

"But I don't know the words to any songs!"

"Yes, you do."

Cuz hope is my melody, my way out of this darkness. "I can't do this," I croak. "I can't."

"You don't have a choice unless you fancy an afternoon swim in the heated pool. I'll play you in after four, okay?" He picks up the guitar and starts tapping his shabby shoes on the crusty blackened surface.

Not a drop of saliva in my throat. I can't get any air in.

A tail emerges out of the raging sea, whipping over our heads by inches and snapping back just as quickly into the impetuous redness.

Heart pounding, skin tightening, I look to the man for help, but he's already lost, swaying his head from side to side, skin a mass of emotive wrinkles as his fingers pluck at the strings.

"Sing as though your life depends on it, kid," he whispers. "One—two—three—"

Only a garbled rasp emerges as I open my mouth. Blood pounds relentlessly in my ears, and I can no longer hear the notes of the guitar. Music Man turns to me and nods, eyes wide and full of urgency. He mouths something, but I hear nothing above the thumping bass of my own blood.

My legs buckle. I feel sick.

The tail emerges from the sea once more, twitching above the froth.

Music Man's eyes grow wider still, but I have nothing. I can't breathe. I want to go home! With tears streaming down my cheeks, warmth spilling down my thigh, I watch the tail begin to whip back.

I look to the man with the guitar one last time, noting the solitary tear that rolls down his right cheek. He offers me a smile and

Stealing Their Future

SJ Townend

I am Mildred March and I don't like much.

I dislike infants; never had any. I despise men; I've never taken a husband. I'm repulsed by young people and most people of a certain age too, all those wants and needs and muddy shoes. I tolerate humans solely at work, knowing I can return to my home alone at the end of a shift. Oh, and I definitely don't like you.

I inherited my disgust for humans from Mother. She used to lock me in my room, tell me I'd the devil in me, try to beat him free from me each night. God, I hated that darned devil; almost as much as I loathed Mother.

There is one thing I do like... one thing I like very much indeed, lots and lots with a cherry on top... and that's the time I get to spend alone with the elderly at the nursing home where I work, once visiting hours are over. I get my chance to tidy away the stagnant, repugnant bags of vintage meat.

***

I've worked at Oak Trees for seventeen years. It pays well. Yes, my basic salary is barely a stone's toss over minimum wage, but I've found a more than comfortable way to turn an extra income over, on the side. If I couldn't supplement in this way, I'd be out of here like a jack rabbit.

Today is cold. I can see ice has collected on the skeletal tree branches like white frosting on finger buns. I'm on reception. At least I get to sit down here, rest my weary bones. I'm only a few years off retirement myself but there's no way you'd catch me paying the extortionate fees my boss charges to live in this utter crock of shit. I'm working around the clock, bringing in all the funds I can to make sure I can look after myself in my own home until I hit the snooze button for the final time. I'll bring a live-in carer in if needs be, but they'll be heavily scrutinised. All kinds get employed here. All kinds. I witness neglectful care everyday with my very own eyes.

I can see a new couple coming up the path. They've parked up a fairly decent car—personalised number plate. Another pair of middle-aged show-offs by the looks.

She's wearing a mink coat. Ah, hang on, she's getting closer, it isn't real—Marks and Spencer's imitation. He's got the waxed jacket, the polished brogues; a copy of that right wing newspaper under his arms—together, they're indistinguishable from every other pair of cunts that visit this joint.

They'll come daily at first, for a week or so. Then they'll make excuses and drop the visits down to once a week. This side of Christmas, it'll be once a month, at best. They'll never write, although they'll say they will and then, in the New Year, it'll be just the annual guilt trip check-in. They'll comment on how much the resident has aged, how they've *deteriorated, hasn't their memory started to fray around the edges.* Heartless bastards.

Before they know it, whichever unlucky sod they've got slammed up in here will have been a resident for five years and cost them the best part of quarter of a million in living costs—most, if not all of the inheritance.

They'll feign surprise when we tell them old Aunt Wendy or gentle Grandpa Bill is to be moved down to the ground floor due to 'mobility issues' or because they 'can't get to the bathroom fast enough' or have 'symptoms of dementia that require round the clock care'.

All of which sees the bills they're probably picking up at this point escalating skywards. *Oh no, please don't hurt me in the money!* they'll say, as they bleed out notes and coins.

The real reason the resident will get moved to the ground floor is because it's one step closer to the basement. The basement is where the morgue is situated. That's where the cool lockers are, the ones which preserve their wrinkled flesh bags until funeral arrangements can be made. Our manager, with a heart of slate, is a shrewd business man. I'm surprised he hasn't applied for planning permission for a crematorium to be built in the car park. He could use the heat it'd generate to warm this place up, save some more pennies.

Ah, they're coming in through the double doors.

I need to open up the guest book, present them with a pen.

"Hello. Welcome to Oak Trees. Is this your first visit?" Of course it is. They're both bloody smiling; both look far too keen to be here.

I do my best 'welcome' smile. The woman's body jerks back slightly. I close my mouth. Damn it. I slide my tongue around my gums. I've forgotten to put in my dentures—a few of my teeth are missing at the front—must've given her a bit of a shock. Ha! Not such a bad morning after all. I'm really grinning now, but I've smacked my lips tight together to conceal my 'offensive grimace'—the boss's words, not mine.

I'm only 62, a spring chicken, but we're all one foot in the grave from the moment we're born. Bodies aren't built to last forever.

"Good morning," It's always the man that speaks first. His name is Tockerton. I see this as he passes me back the guest book. "We've come to see Mrs Tockerton, my mother. She arrived yesterday. On the second floor, room 58, I believe."

"Ah yes, lovely Judith Tockerton," I reply, leading them along the corridor. I play with the rusty razor blade in my pocket as we walk along, seeing how far under my nail bed I can slide it without it hurting too much.

We rattle through the old building, bowling balls thundering along the return gulley, towards the 'entertainment' room. It stinks of boiled cabbage, sulphur and urine. All the rooms do here. "Sorry about the smell, we're having problems with the drains."

"I see," Mr T replies. Mrs T is holding a satin handkerchief over her nose. The old biddies don't

27

care about the pong. Most of them are so heavily doped up; you could drag a rotten whale carcass right through, smeared in fresh pig excrement. They wouldn't bat an eyelid.

I see Judith over by the television. "There we go, in between Arthur and Olive." I contemplate trying to describe the wrinklies sat either side of Judith to give them more direction, but they all look the same to me. Reptilian, paper thin skin, sunken eyes like clouded marbles lost at sea, white hair that needs dusting away. "They're watching Gone with the Wind. How lovely," I say.

Of course they're watching Gone with the Wind. It's on repeat all day every Tuesday. And Friday. Old Rupert tried to change the channel last week. He'd somehow gotten hold of the remote. The batteries in it went flat months ago. I'd caught him with it and put it back on the top shelf where none of the folded oldies can reach. He said he liked the way the buttons felt, but if he had a remote control they'd all want one. There's no way the boss would bust the budget for toys.

"Thank you. What was your name?" Mr T asks. He's looking for my name badge. Looks like I'd forgotten to put that on this morning too.

"Mildred," I reply. "Mildred March. I'll be in the staff kitchen over the way if you need me," I say and leave them to it. I've just time to look Judith up on the computer system, see what I'm working with before deciding if it's worth listening in to their conversation. I find the notes from her GP.

28

At the grand age of ninety-three, Judith has 'good mental faculties' and has sold up her family home in the Lake District to spend her golden years at Oak Trees. Judith is a widow, former librarian and former treasurer of her local spiritualist church. Judith's family have chosen Oak Trees for her. Judith is on 20mg Simvastatin for blood pressure, 2 x 20mg Omeprazole for acid reflux, benzodiazepine is to be taken when necessary for sleep-related wellbeing. She has a history of treatment for dissociative-identity disorder, which is to be managed with 15mg Clozapine, twice daily. Judith likes cats and French pastries.

So, the old windbag has a penny or two, a history of poor mental health and, at age 92, she's also quite frankly, living on borrowed time. The computer system is great, although I couldn't give a shit about her former life. I've already had the pleasure of changing her adult nappy this morning, already wiped shit—of the wet and nugget variety—from her saggy, growling undercarriage. I feel like we know each other intimately already.

***

I tiptoe back. Outside of the entertainment room, I press my ear against the wall and listen in. I tend to observe the family with their elderly relative for at least a couple of visits before offering additional services.

"I still hear the voices," Judith murmurs. I peek round the door jamb and spot Mr and Mrs T giving each other a concerned glance. "I'm still channelling."

"We've talked about this before," Mr T says. His brow furrows. "It's your hearing aid. You've got to clean it. You're getting feedback or something."

"Picking up radio stations, I expect," Mrs T attempts a joke but it literally falls on deaf ears.

"What, dear?" Judith says, raising and placing a shaking arm on her daughter-in-law's knee. Mrs T is repulsed by this contact. I can see it in her body language. She hates the old bag. Excellent.

"I spoke to your father last week," Judith stammers.

"Mother, Father's been dead for years now. Stop with this nonsense," Mr T replies. He's thinking he should take his mother's hand in his, show a little compassion, work it for the inheritance that he knows is coming his way soon, but he's as repulsed by the old maid's yellow-blue-grey skeletal knuckles as his wife is and I can see he decides against it. "Come now, we've talked about this before. Have you been taking your tablets? Myself and Dawn, we don't believe in all this supernatural poppycock."

This is fascinating to watch. The old bag is already showing clear signs of mental decline, most likely significant dementia and she's only been in a week. Should be a fast journey to the ground floor. I'll need to act quickly.

"How's the food?" Mrs T is trying to change the subject.

The food here is atrocious. Same grey slop every day. Occasionally, fruit's offered, but only occasionally. We try to keep the old gits bunged up rather than loose—much easier to keep clean. Guests aren't allowed in at meal times, so no-one is any the wiser. If they complain, we mention dementia. *How could they possibly have forgotten the delicious roast and cherry Bakewell that was served yesterday? And what do they mean, 'there's no entertainment'? We had a comedian and a singing group in last week and the local scouts popped by on Sunday to play checkers with them.*

It's the perfect storm here. The perfect storm.

"The food? Did you say food, Barbara?"

"Yes, Judith. The food. How's the food?"

"I thought you said: 'how's your mood'," Judith replies.

"How *is* your mood?" Mr T asks.

"Oh, breakfast was awful," Judith says. "I haven't opened my bowels since I got here."

"Is that the time?" Mr T says. There's no clock in here. This place is timeless. He's not looking at a watch or his phone either.

Neither of them want to be here. This is looking hopeful.

"Judith's looking tired," I say as I glide into the room with a forced, closed-lip smile. It's time to guide them to the exit, not before asking a few questions, to ensure I'm barking up the right tree.

I wave them off and catch the end of their conversation as they head to their car.

"We did the right thing, getting her in here, even though it costs so much. She'll have a much better final innings here than at home, won't she?" Mrs T says.

"Those relentless kids egging her windows, leaving bags of human faeces on her doorstep, shouting at her and calling her an evil witch can't have been very nice. Not forgetting what they did to her cat. I'm sure she's better off here." He's looking back up to see if he can see her looking out of the window. He won't.

"Yes. That's what tipped her over the edge, the cat."

***

People are predictable. I observe the Tockertons and their declining frequency of visits over the following months. I leave time for them to receive at least two bills in the post. Mr T is in charge of Judith's estate. He's in charge of making the payments to Oak Trees, from the old crone's savings. Each cheque he writes will sting, even though it's not (yet) his money. I've seen it before, many times. I know when to pounce.

***

It's January and as bleak as death outside. The residents I'm watching today in the lounge look like they've all had droopy grey clay flung at their faces. Jowls, protruding hair where it shouldn't be and not where it should, nasty, stained lap blankets, bunions pointing east and west out of gaps in their sandals. If it wasn't for the perks, I wouldn't stomach this much living decay and stench day in, day out.

I see Mr and Mrs Tockerton walking up the path. It's time I spoke with them. Judith shat the bed this morning. Muggins here had to clean it up. She needs to go down a level; I've seen Tracy has already filled out the paperwork. Need to move fast, close the deal.

I place a naked plastic baby in her arms which she hugs tightly. This usually does the job.

"Hello, Mr and Mrs Tockerton. How lovely to see you. It's been—"

"Hello, Mildred. It's been a month or so hasn't it. Lovely Christmas?" Urgh, rhetoric. They couldn't give a damn about my Christmas. They won't be staying in touch with me once Judith's snuffed it. They can barely be arsed to keep in touch with their own family. I'll be another blank face in the street in under a year, just another anonymous bastard to compete with for parking spaces in the town centre.

I lie. "Yes, delightful. Spent it with family. It's all about the little ones, isn't it? How are your lovely grandchildren?"

What a load of bollocks. The only way I'd spend Christmas with a child would be if it was small enough to fit in the oven and tasted good with cranberry sauce.

They spill rehashed stories about their perfect grandchildren. I try to hold down the vomit and bile collecting in my stomach. I think about what I'm going to do later instead. It brings a sardonic grin back to my chops.

33

Mrs T is looking over at Judith with the same look of concern she has every time she visits, when Judith starts talking in the different voices. It's been getting worse. I'll not lie to them if they ask. In fact, I'll make sure to mention how much she's declined. It'll only work to my favour.

"Why's Judith holding a doll?" Mrs T has taken the bait.

"Lots of our residents like to hold dolls, especially the women. Especially as they climb a little further down that sad ladder of memory loss. Reminds them of holding their own wee ones," I say.

I'm smiling too much. I'm practically salivating at how well I'm drawing them in. Hook, line and sinker. I need to tone it down so I think about Mother.

Mrs T looks perturbed. Bingo.

"Her mind's getting worse? Since our last visit?"

"Afraid so. They're making space for her downstairs, she needs monitoring more closely."

"On the dementia floor?" Mr T interjects.

" Afraid so." I feign sympathy. It burns like holy water.

I know exactly what's coming next. He'll talk money. He'll want to know how much this transition will hurt his pocket.

"So... will that cost more?"

"The fees will be a little over double what you're currently paying. They require so much more care downstairs, you see. Isn't it such a terrible decline?"

"Is she still hearing the voices?" Mrs T asks in almost a whisper.

I explain to the Tockertons how I've walked into her room to find her completely away with the fairies on many an occasion.

"She holds full court with her dead relatives. Brian, her mother, father, her sister. She talks at length with her cat," I say, "And with a few others I've not heard either of you mention."

Many of the old cabbage-breath bastards talk to the dead as they approach the final door holding back the white light—it's not unusual—doesn't make it any less peculiar to witness though. Mother used to chat with Satan all the time, whilst she was beating him from me.

Judith in particular has very clear 'visions' when impersonating her dead relatives. Most of what comes out of the old farts' mouths I ignore, though. Waste of my time, listening to their stories about the war, about the pain in their joints, about the animals and children they've lost. Blah blah blah.

"She does like to chat," I continue, "and her incontinence is becoming an increasing concern too."

I lead them to Judith and make my excuses. Listening in from the corridor, I plan my pitch.

They talk to each other over her head, as if she isn't there. I suppose, in a way she isn't. When she does speak, it's usually as or to someone else and rarely makes any sense.

35

"Such an awful waste. Look at her," Mr T says, picking lint from his trousers, "She's a shell of the woman she was."

"We could've bought that property in Marbella for what we've spent already," Mrs T whispers. She crosses her arms and stares at Judith. "She's mumbling away, staring out at the lawn... doesn't even know we're here."

I watch Judith turn her head and cock it to one side. I've seen her do this before. She's about to pretend to be her husband. It's quite amusing even though it's probably a result of her brain slowly eating itself up, congealing whilst still pulsing weakly with some sort of basic life.

"Don't you dare, you silly bitch," Judith says. That one even caught me by surprise. I've never heard her speak so loudly before, let alone swear. I chuckle in the corridor and cup my hand over my mouth. I don't want them to catch me eaves-dropping—it could blow this ship out of the water.

"Who's she talking to?" asks Mrs T. "She doesn't sound like her anymore."

"No. Judith has gone," Mr T says. "And so has the money."

"Nearly," Mrs T says. "There's still about 300k left."

I take this as my cue and walk back into the entertainment lounge with cups of tea and a plate of biscuits for my two special visitors. With my tongue, I check I've put my best teeth in and give them my most endearing smile. It feels like dripping acid in my own eyes.

36

"Mr and Mrs T, I'm terribly sorry, but I couldn't help overhearing the tail end of your conversation. I'm so sorry for the way things are progressing with your mother. Such an awful way to go, isn't it? I was wondering if you'd be interested in having a little chat."

"It's awful," he replies, overegging his sandwich, "Such a terrible, terrible descent."

I chat with them briefly about their grandchildren. Again. The eldest is considering university. 'Oh aren't the fees so expensive, wouldn't it be nice to help them out', and 'wouldn't the children benefit with some additional money towards their mortgages?' And 'isn't it a shame to be throwing good money to a care home for an individual who's perhaps... already checked out?'

I tell them to call me if they'd like things to *speed up a little* and I pass them a card with my number on it. Mr T accepts it, although they both look a little taken aback by my offers. This, I anticipate. They'd have to be complete psychopaths for it to not knock them slightly sideways, wouldn't it?

The cogs in their brains are considering the implications of my gentle suggestions and the calculator parts are processing how much money they'll save if they accept my offer.

Sometimes, with particularly unhappy families, I offer a selection of 'endings'—you'd be surprised at how often people don't always choose the most humane.

***

It's Thursday morning. The Wizard of Oz is on repeat. I know the script off by heart. Judith is staring at the screen like it's the first time she's ever seen it. I'll get to Judith shortly. First, the boss has asked me to address old Arthur's stinking bedsore.

I wheel the medical trolley over, roll on a fresh pair of latex gloves, wrap a fabric bandage up his leg and cut it with the medical scissors. Then I wheel the trolley over to Judith.

She's asleep. I shake her hard and pinch the skin on the back of her arm. There's a vacancy in her eyes. Yet there's also a spark within them still when she speaks. It's a spark I've not seen in anyone else before. And, I'll not lie, it's quite unnerving.

The money's been transferred and I'm eager to fulfil my half of the deal.

I've been collecting her prescription meds for the last few weeks, withholding them. I pull out a handful of the red and purple pills, tip them into a cup on the trolley, crush them with the back of a spoon and stir them into her soup. It's never enough to kill them, just slows the heart right down, ensures they can't be brought back if one of the do-gooders find them.

I crouch beside her and feed her from a spoon. I'm not sure what smells worse, her rancid breath or the spiked slop I'm shovelling into her trap hole. No-one else is around, they're all dealing with Maude who's got herself stuck in the bath or are bunking off by the fire exit, chaining Lisa's duty free cigarettes.

She refuses to eat. I pinch her nose tightly until her jaw slackens. I turn my head away at the odour that emanates—she's already rotting from the inside. This one stinks worse than any I've dealt with before. I force her to chug the lukewarm meal down and slap her on the cheek for luck.

I take a handful of napkins and hold them tight over her mouth until she swallows the last of her dinner. The cheeky cow tries to bite me. She has more teeth than I do—it hurts. Naughty old mare. I give her another slap; think about bringing the razor blade out from my pocket. A beige rivulet of soup dribbles from the corner of her mouth. I let it drop into her lap. She's cowering back in her chair. Should be easy money this one, she's a slight string bean of a witch.

I turn to search for a firm cushion. I'm not going to use my hands to exterminate this one, she's a biter.

I turn back round. Judith has somehow hauled her sorry arse up and out of her chair. She's hobbled over to the medical trolley. Is she trying to make a run for it? I cackle loudly. Old Arthur wakes from his afternoon nap and stares at me with stupid, sunken eyes. He won't remember any of this. Even if he does, he's an unreliable narrator.

Firm cushion in my hand, I march over to my pay-check and grab her arm. I grab so hard, it snaps or it pulls out from its joint and I curse. Now I'm going to have to make this look like a fall. Damn these wrinkled gits with their fossilised bird bones, joints looser than broken waistbands. As I think about which way to push her, I see she's hiding something in her other hand. She grabs my arm with her other hand and her face is now up close to mine. Her eyes are rolling back into her head.

She shouts at me in a deep voice: "You silly bitch, Mildred. You stupid little girl. You've the devil in you."

Mother's voice.

This old witch Judith is speaking at me with Mother's voice, wearing Mother's words like a suit of armour and a sword. Her body is growing hotter and hotter. I see steam blasting from her ears as her whole head starts to shake side-to-side. Her words are coming out faster. She's spitting as she shouts.

"You bitch girl, the devil's in you."

It's too late. I don't see the scissors she's grabbed from the trolley in time. She's plunging them deep in me. Stainless steel slides through my skin, belly fat, stomach. She pulls them out and shoves them back in again and again. I scream in pain. Blood and stomach acid spray out of my guts like the smoke that spilt from the incense burner that swung down the aisle of the church at Mother's funeral. My nostrils fill with the memory of frankincense and the care-home blended stench of stale piss and coppery blood.

Red is everywhere: carpet, cushion which I've dropped to the floor, Judith, me.

She comes at me again, harder, firmer, with the angry energy of Mother before she died, with the voice of Mother in her mouth and she stabs me with the silvery blades until there's nowhere left to perforate.

I drop to my knees, flop over on my side and whack my head on the edge of the medical trolley. My head splits open. In and out the scissor blades keep going, puncture after puncture. She jams them in and drags them across, my clothes have been shredded and flaps of my flesh are hanging down. My intestines are bulging out like moist, purple inner tubes. I'm lying on the floor, my heart is racing fast but pumping weakly. Blood is gushing out from my body, leaving my poor heart with less and less to squeeze on. I look up at Judith. She's wiping off the handle of the scissors and placing them back on the trolley. Is she laughing at me? Are they all laughing at me, all the old, rumpled fuckers? All aware they've slipped the net this time, got away from my fatal hands?

My field of view is dimming at the edges; the light is shrinking, like at the end of an old cartoon or the view out from the top of the well that I think I'm plummeting down. Immeasurable pain jars through every inch of my pin-cushioned body. I vomit. It sprays out in front of me, a warm mixture of scrambled egg and blood, a violently offensive puddle of punishment which collects around my head for my final seconds on earth.

I see only Judith's fuzzy outline now, only one of my eyes are above the pool of sick—she's sitting back down in her chair. She's clicking her shoulder back into place. She's dabbing at the blood from her blouse with a moistened tissue. She's tutting at me as she mops. She's staring at me with my mother's eyes.

Blackness.

41

Party Monsters

Lena Ng

It was hot so I was sitting out on the porch. The house across from me seemed to be empty no more. It was a two-storey with a black roof and shutters, the windows on either side positioned to look like gaping eyes on an empty face. Enough time had passed that no one spoke of the tragedy that left it abandoned and cars no longer slowed down to stare. Last Thursday, I saw a U-Haul pull up to the driveway and furniture—mahogany armoires and china hutches, a silver chandelier, velvet-covered dining room chairs, pieces you would imagine furnishing a crumbling castle—being brought in.

Today I saw the new neighbour bustling about in her garden and thought it was a good opportunity to introduce myself. She was crouched over five terracotta pots, feeding her plants with a pair of tweezers. "Howdy, neighbour," she proclaimed in a hearty singer's voice. She wore her thick, black hair in a coil on the top of her head. "You wouldn't have any rotting meat, would you? These things eat a ton."

Truthfully, the plants were gobbling up the pink-blackened bits as fast she could feed them. They licked with their giant, scarlet-spotted tongues and though I couldn't see any eyes, they seemed to be scrutinizing me.

42

"I have some leftovers. Will they do?" The plants seemed like such fascinating, albeit greedy, things, with giant, lusciously magnificent blooms, red like the kiss of a vampire.

She tickled a carnivorous blossom under its chin, which made it scrunch up its petals. "Darling *Dionaea trappus giganticus*. I breed them, you know. Best sellers on Etsy." The blossom stretched open for another mottled morsel plucked from a Tupperware container. "I leave the meat in the sun until it's good and rancid. Wouldn't want the poor dears to get indigestion."

I returned a short time later with a hunk of pot-roast which she accepted with a grateful smile. "Say," she said, plunking the roast into the dirt of the flower bed, "I'm having a party on Saturday. Why don't you come by?"

I'm not usually fond of people or parties, but curiosity about the new neighbours and the peculiar history of the house prompted me to say 'yes' without thinking. The house's odd stories had changed over the years: some said there were stairs leading into the ceiling; others spoke of hidden rooms with doors camouflaged by wallpaper; tabloids once reported of maze-like corridors folding in on themselves. One rumour was that the original owner believed she would die when she stopped construction so rooms were added in a haphazard fashion which moved about like blocks in a Rubik's Cube. The strangest story was about doors leading to alien dimensions where other-worldly creatures dwelt, a yarn concocted by a bug-eyed alcoholic who was later hauled off to the nearby asylum.

Saturday came around and I crossed the crumbling, deserted road to the neighbour's house with another old pot-roast. The vault-like door creaked open a crack. The neighbour looked resplendent in a midnight dress which draped over every hairpin curve, topped off with an extravagant fur stole. Her eye shadow was the colour of sparkly bruises. I held out the chunk of meat, which was wrapped in brown parchment, with a bottle of red wine. "Thanks for having me, uh—"

"Hortensia."

"I'm Bernice."

"Welcome," she said and flung open the door. The house seemed unnaturally larger inside. The living room, cathedral sized with a high ceiling, was festooned with streamers and balloons. The party-goers came in all forms and sizes: tiny as a mouse, large as a house, some sizes in between. A big sign reading "Happy Birthday" hung on the far wall.

My face fell at the sign. "I didn't realize... I would have brought a present."

Hortensia fluttered her delicate hands around me. "No, no," she assured me. "Absolutely no need. Your presence is the present." She manoeuvred me through the throng. Guests were milling about sipping, nibbling, flirting. One man, in a slim-fitting summer suit, danced a three-legged jig.

"Over here, Carl," she said, waving her elegant, crimson-manicured hand. "Come meet our neighbour, Bernice."

"Wonderful," exclaimed Carl, a debonair gentleman with a toothy Cheshire-cat smile under a fine-looking moustache, bumping his way through. "Just in time for the games." He led me by the arm to a group of laughing guests. "We're playing pin the tail."

The tail he handed to me, skewered to the end of a dagger, was still squirming. "Go on," he urged, placing his large hand on the small of my back. "Don't be squeamish."

The thing I was supposed to pin it on didn't look like it would cooperate. It glared at me with three of its eyes. I edged away, holding the squirming tail away from me. "It already has a tail. Two, in fact."

"That's the fun," Carl replied, as the other guests giggled. "Getting another one on there."

He spun me around and gave me a shove while I made a half-hearted stab at what I thought was a bottom. Finally, I jabbed the dagger onto the wall where the hairless tail flailed and thumped, spasming like a beheaded snake over the purple-blotched wallpaper. "Oops, missed," I said, as brightly as I could muster. "Who's next?"

A man with a perky bow tie and bright red suspenders got up to take my place. He spun four times, stabbed and the tail was embedded in the side of a gelatinous flank. The ensuing roar was tooth-rattling. With an unexpected quickness, the man scootered away, dodging the claws.

I sat on the corner of the blush-pink, chintz settee. "Whose birthday is it anyway?" I whispered to another party goer who was sitting with ankles crossed on the couch. She held a large lump of food on a paper plate.

The guest, an elderly lady with a smear of coral lipstick, hair tinted with a blue rinse, put a liver-spotted hand to her mouth. "You don't know?"

I shook my head.

She gave me a gap-toothed smile. "Imagine going to a birthday party and not knowing whose birthday it is. Hey, Horace, come listen to this."

"Shhhh," I said, mortified. "Forget I asked."

The lady speared the lump as it attempted to ooze off the plate. She sniffed in a snooty way. "Party hasn't even started yet. When's he going to get here?"

"Piñata time," Carl announced, after the thing with five tails scuttled to the ceiling out of everyone's reach. With a magician's flair, he pulled away the covering blanket to reveal the piñata with its numerous arms and heads. It was glossily painted and had such awful, accusing stares.

The first guest, a ten-year-old girl with a braid to her waist, was handed a spiked mace. She was spun around and around and flailed the mace wildly. A hooting, enthusiastic guest holding a pewter beer stein—after a spike to the eye—learned to stay out of the way. A lady wearing a short sequined dress didn't have much luck with swinging a scimitar while another whipped five-pointed shuriken all around the room. The writhing piñata, despite the rope, was adept at dodging.

Finally my turn arrived. I was handed what looked like an axe on top of a stick, which at my confused look, they told me was called a halberd.

Carl wrapped a blindfold around my eyes and gave me a winding spin. With the delighted shrieks of 'watch out', 'duck' and 'get out of the way' ringing around me, I hit the target with a sounding thwack. I felt flesh give way and I was showered in liquid both slimy and sticky.

When Carl took off the blindfold, I saw I was covered in green goo. I guess the jellied heart which twitched at my feet was supposed to be the prize. The room continued to spin, as though I stood in the centre of a top. The floor whizzed around and around me while the four corners of the room flew by in a dizzying blur. When it came to an abrupt stop, I was in another room. Instead of purple-blotched wallpaper, it was red. The pinned wiggling tail had disappeared. The cathedral ceiling was also gone and in its place, a low-hanging, wooden one.

And, inexplicably, there was no door.

I tried to walk, lilting to the side as though I were on sea legs and managed to bump into Carl, my nose glancing off the side of his shoulder. I gripped his arm and looked into his bat-black eyes. "Happy birthday, by the way."

Carl frowned and his handsome face darkened into something more sinister. "It's not my birthday."

"Hortensia's?" I glanced in her direction, but had to quickly look away. She was now wearing little aside from a necklace of teeth.

"No, no. The guest of honour has yet to arrive." In a series of guttural sounds, Carl spoke some words which weren't in a language I recognized, deep-voiced as though something was emerging from within. It made the hair stand up on the back of my neck.

The sounds made my head start to throb. I put my fingers to my temples. "I think I have to go," I slurred. The floor began tilting and rising stomach acid burned my throat. I placed my hands on the walls which seemed to pulse inward. The ceiling emitted a grinding creak as it started to lower. I made an effort to lurch my way around the room in search of a door.

"Don't be silly," Carl said, but I managed to sidestep his grasp. The laughter grew louder and high-pitched and seemed to come from within the walls and floorboards. Like a blind woman, I searched with my fingertips for any cracks in the red-blotted wallpaper. When I felt a seam, I pushed open the wall. With my breath in a sharp staccato, I stumbled into a pitch-black corridor. The section of wall closed behind me in a spring-loaded slam. I put my hand on something soft and squelchy and flinched away before it could eat at my skin. Shaking and grasping, I trudged in what felt like thick, bubbling mud. My legs burned as the ground seemed to swallow my feet. I moved with a cornered animal's instinct, needing to escape from this dreadful house and its occupants.

The ground shifted and grew more solid and I heard the pounding of pursuing footsteps behind me. In a blind panic, I slammed into a wall, realized I had come to a T-junction and swerved right. I saw the outline of a door, the frame illuminated in glowing green phosphorescence. I yanked the door open and winced at the brightness of the light, stumbling back at the smell of ripened road kill. The buzzing drone of blue-bottles filled my ears. Silhouetted in the door frame was a tangled mass of talon-studded tentacles and slavering double jaws.

The pounding footsteps came to a halt. The guests circled behind me. Slowly, they dropped to the ground. With noses to the floor, they prostrated before the glowing doorway and the terrible thing emerging from it. I've never seen so many eyes. In chanting crescendo, the melody of "Happy Birthday" arose around me. In awed tones, Hortensia's operatic soprano rose sweetly above the others, mingling with the droning buzz of the flies. Even the reedy, alien-sounding voices of the carnivorous plants joined in, scarlet-spotted tongues snapping into the air.

The bile of horror choked me and I backed away from glowing door. I realized I was wearing little other than a necklace of teeth. I tried to flee when—

"Oh no," said Carl with a jovial wink, winding my mouth shut with a wide polka-dotted ribbon before trussing me up like a turkey. "You can't leave now." The bright light illuminated the curve of his horns. He popped a jaunty purple bow onto the top of my head. "You're the present."

A Demonic Dip

John Cady

When Rory, the eldest of the Cretin boys, went to the basement to check on his youngest brother, Will, he nearly dropped to his knees in despair when he realized Will was nowhere to be found.

"Will! Where the hell are you?"

He didn't bother paying much attention to his surroundings. He was sure his younger, more curious brother had ventured into the back room. He wasn't supposed to go in. He was only supposed to guard it. Those were his father's orders.

Jacob Cretin introduced each of his boys to that door once they were old enough to handle the responsibility of guarding it without peeking. Eventually, he'd let them see what was in there. There was a lock on it at one point, but someone lost the key along the way, so he had to bust it off one night with a hammer and leave it that way. Besides, it would have been a hassle if they kept on having to find the key every time they brought a woman down there to hand her over.

"Will?" Rory shouted, again. This time his brother stumbled down the bulkhead stairs and into the basement. He was just finishing zipping his fly up when he entered.

"Rory!" he blurted out, nervous as hell. *"You won't tell Dad, will you?"*

Rory was confused.

"Tell him what exactly?"

"That I stepped away from my post to take a leak. I swear I'd have pissed my pants if I'd had stuck around any longer."

Rory breathed a sigh, part agitated and part relieved. He was agitated that baby brother was careless enough to leave the door unattended for any amount of time, but relieved that he hadn't gone inside to have a look for himself. He knew that when you do that, there's a good chance you don't come out the same – and he thought too highly of Will to wish that on him. Plus, who knows how their old man would have responded?

"Mind if I hang out down here for a smoke or two?" Rory asked as he pulled a pack of cigarettes from his pocket. He was planning on it regardless, but he figured he'd ask out of common courtesy.

"I don't need a babysitter," Will grumbled. Of all his family members, he knew Rory had had the least exposure to whatever was on the other side of that door. The others were too far gone to even care if he had gone in there to see for himself. *Hell!* They'd have probably treated it like he'd lost his virginity. Not Rory, though. He honestly wouldn't have minded if Will never made his way in there. He didn't care for this particular rite of passage.

"I'm not here to babysit you," he explained. "If that's what it seems like, then I can leave. I don't need to stick around."

Will thought about it.

"Nah," he finally said, only slightly annoyed. "You can stay. I could use the company. I've got another two hours to go."

51

They sat in silence for the next five minutes or so as Rory puffed away on his cigarette. He occasionally stole a glance at his little brother. His gaze never stayed there too long, though, for fear that Will would catch him staring.

"I'm surprised you haven't asked me yet," he said, finally breaking his silence.

"What's the use?" Will replied. "You never tell me anyways."

"True."

Will sighed. He didn't see the rationale in spending hours guarding a door he himself wouldn't be able to enter for some time – especially when it was right downstairs from where he slept. "What kind of sense did that make?"

"Seriously, though, can't you just tell me? I'm going to find out eventually – when Dad thinks I'm of the proper age, I guess. I mean, I've been losing sleep over it. That ain't healthy. At least, if I know, I won't be kept awake wondering about it every night. Right?"

Rory rolled his eyes. His little brother was relentless. It ran in the family.

"There's nothing but evil on the other side of this door," he explained. "And, it's not the kind of evil you'd find anywhere out here."

Will wasn't following. Rory could see it in his eyes.

"There's a well in there; or, maybe it's a pool. I don't know. All I know is if you find yourself in its water, then you'll find yourself changing – for the worse. Dad thinks it's a portal to the underworld or something. Whatever's in that water isn't in any of the other water we've been in. He thinks there might be demons involved."

"Demons?" Will said, chuckling beneath his breath. "Nah. There's no such things as demons. You're just messing with me."

Rory simply shrugged his shoulders.

"I swear I'm not," he replied. "I swear on Mom's grave I'm telling the truth."

Will immediately stopped laughing and his face took on a grave expression. Talk of their mother was forbidden in the house. That was another of Dad's rules.

"Really?" he asked, and then gave the door a long look of fright. A chill ran up his spine. He thought about all of the times he'd seen either his father or one of his brothers drag a woman kicking and screaming down into that basement, then heard that door slam shut, only to hear it swing open once again shortly thereafter and see the same woman emerge from the basement door happy as can be.

"And, the women they've brought in with them?" he asked. "What happened to them in there?"

Rory looked at his brother with sorrowful eyes. He started to wish he hadn't gone down to check on him. This all could have been avoided for a little while longer.

"They were led into the water," he explained.

"*Led* in?" Will asked, pressing him.

"Okay, forced in," Rory said, correcting himself.

"And, then what happened? They weren't drowned. I know that much."

Rory shook his head. The poor things probably would have preferred being drowned.

"No. They weren't. They were possessed by something. That's how Dad tells it anyways. And, from what I've seen, I think he might be right. Something bad definitely happened to them in there. Only, none of them seemed too broken up over it afterwards. I always thought maybe Dad did something to them in there and it made me sick to my stomach. He swears on Mom's grave he didn't, though. He just got them into the water and the water took over."

Poor Will was dumbfounded. He couldn't have possibly dreamt this scenario up. Sure, he thought there was something sinister going on in there, but he never imagined it involved demons.

"Have *you* ever been in the water?" he finally asked. He had to know.

"Only once," Rory admitted. "It felt great at the time; but, that feeling soon wore off and I felt this massive wave of guilt sweep right over me. I knew I never wanted to experience that sensation again. I thought about Mom and what she might think of all this. She'd hate it. In fact, it would have probably driven her away. The others have all been in there plenty of times like it's some goddamn Jacuzzi or something. I think Dad's been in there the most. He can't seem to get enough of it and that alone scares the hell out of me."

As if on cue, the basement door swung open and their father stumbled down the stairs with some woman slung over his shoulder, kicking and screaming. Each son slid his chair to the side as Jacob wrenched the door open and carried her in.

"*Please, help me*," she whimpered on her way past.

They did their best to ignore her plea.

Rory noticed Will trying to steal a glimpse of what was about to go down in there and quickly pushed the door shut. Will looked at him, disappointed.

Moments later, both Jacob and the woman emerged from the room. Both were soaking wet and grinning.

Will watched his father help the woman up the stairs as though they had just returned from a night of drinking. She fought to stifle nervous laughter throughout their climb. In her mind, it was clear she was up to no good.

He gave the door to the back room a long, hard look. He was teetering back and forth on whether or not to just take it upon himself to venture in without the green light from his old man. Surely, he'd understand.

"Don't do it," his older brother said, ever the angel upon his shoulder. He knew just what he was thinking because he himself had also thought it plenty of times.

"It isn't worth it," he added. He was right, too. It wasn't. He'd been in there the one time and that was only because his father had insisted. He'd already seen the damage it had done to his father and brothers. It was like a drug – only it was worse because it had a mind of its own. It sought vessels, and the old man was more than happy to deliver them.

He often wondered about the women his dad had kidnapped and brought down there. More specifically, he wondered what happened once he released them back into the world. Did they ever recover from the experience? Or, did the evil stay with them for the duration?

"Why are you still here?" Will felt bold enough to ask.

"To make sure you don't go in there," Rory replied, matter-of-factly. No point in keeping up the charade.

"I don't just mean right now – tonight," Will explained. "I mean..."

"I don't either," Rory replied, cutting him off. "Honestly, I'm trying to keep you from ever going in there."

Will couldn't believe his ears. There was no way in hell his father was going to allow this to happen. This was a mutiny of sorts.

"Dad will never go for that," Will noted. "You know that, right? It's like going into the family business."

Rory quickly dismissed this.

"That's a hell of a way to put it," he said. "This sure as hell isn't some family business. It's kidnapping and whatever the hell you call that in there. It isn't a business. That's for damn sure. We're not turning a profit. We're turning these women into vessels of evil and I sure as hell don't want any part in it. I don't want you to be involved either."

Will could see the sincerity in his older brother's eyes. He meant every word of it. If need be, he was willing to risk it all to protect him.

"Let's leave then," he suggested.

Rory was taken aback.

"*Leave?* As in never come back?"

Will nodded. It was exactly what he meant. He knew they wouldn't be able to keep this up forever. It just wasn't feasible.

"We can leave right now," he continued. "I haven't seen the other guys all night, and Dad – well, he's clearly busy. We can duck right out through the bulkhead and we're gone. I mean, shit, they might not even come looking for us."

Rory smirked.

"Tell me I'm wrong."

Rory chuckled.

"I don't know that you are wrong. I would hope they'd come looking for us eventually, but who knows with Dad? He obviously isn't the same guy that wouldn't so much as miss one of our little league games."

"Exactly," Will said, with a half-hearted smile. "I say we do it."

"Maybe we should," Rory replied, with a shrug of his shoulders. He knew in the long run this was probably their best option if they ever wanted a halfway normal life. It was better to escape while they had the chance, he figured. He had to admit he was impressed with his younger brother for orchestrating such a bold manoeuvre. He knew he could be conniving, but he always figured he used that talent for getting out of his chores – nothing serious like this.

"Lead the way," Will insisted.

Rory nodded and then climbed the bulkhead stairs. He turned to give the basement one last look, brushing up against his brother in the process. He faced forward once again and gently pushed the bulkhead door open. He then stepped out into the night air. He was free. He could already feel it.

In seconds, the door slammed shut behind him and he could hear Will hurrying back down the stairs. It was a ruse. He'd been tricked.

"*No!*" he shouted, banging feverishly on the door. "*What are you doing?*"

He eventually pried the door open and hurried down the stairs. The door to the back room had already been opened by the time he arrived.

"*Will!*" he shouted, hoping it would jar his brother from his clouded judgment.

He hurried into the room, but he was too late for there, soaking it all in was his younger brother. All that remained of him above the surface was his head. His maniacal grin would forever be etched in Rory's mind. All his older brother could do for him anymore was weep.

Endurance

R.G. Evans

"Five minutes, Mr. Goldman."

Goldman raised one hand--half acknowledgment, half dismissal—but didn't even glance at the production assistant as she leaned through the green room doorway. He was bathed in flickering, silvery light, keeping his face toward the TV monitor up on the wall, eyes transfixed on the dark-suited man on the screen, leaning forward in his chair like Goldman himself, the man studying the objects arrayed on the table in front of him.

Five minutes, Goldman thought. *After a lifetime, five minutes!*

The green room door opened and closed again. Goldman felt a familiar pair of hands on his shoulders and then the tissue bib from makeup being pulled from around his neck.

"You won't need this out there, Papi," the man whispered into Goldman's ear. "You don't want to look like a fool in your big moment, eh?"

Goldman turned away from the monitor at last and smiled up at Hernan. His beautiful, bottomless eyes. His full lips. His impossibly lustrous black hair. Goldman lay his hand atop Hernan's.

"My big moment," he said. "It's truly here, isn't it?"

"Yes, Papi, it's here." Hernan leaned down again to Goldman and kissed him on the cheek, the tip of his tongue tracing the whorls of Goldman's ear. "And so am I."

Goldman felt the blood rising in his cheeks. He closed his eyes and leaned his head back against the reassuring tautness of Hernan's belly. When he opened his eyes again, he saw the man on the screen had leaned back in his chair, shaking his head almost imperceptibly. But Goldman saw it and smiled.

And felt himself growing hard.

The door opened again and the production assistant said, "We're ready for you, Mr. Goldman."

Goldman drew a deep breath and rose from the chair. He turned toward Hernan and saw the younger man smile.

"You won't be needing this out there either, Papi," Hernan said, cupping Goldman's crotch in one hand. "You save this for after, eh? Save it for Mykonos."

Goldman blushed and smiled at Hernan, then kissed him once lightly on the lips. "Wish me luck," he said.

"You of all people know there's no such thing. And even if there was, you know you wouldn't need it. Go out there and crucify him."

***

He knows, Goldman thought as he entered the studio. *He knows this is the end.*

In the heat and unforgiving lights, Kessler already looked like a man defeated. Gone were the

60

cocky smirk and swaggering posture. In their place, Goldman saw a thin sheen of sweat on Kessler's upper lip, a nervousness about his eyes. *I almost feel sorry for him*, Goldman thought.

Almost.

Goldman took his seat on the dais, but neither he nor Kessler acknowledged the other's presence. Instead, Goldman looked down at the table he'd watched Kessler study from the green room. The assortment of metal vials. A collection of spoons and spatulas. Three wristwatches and a pocket watch with a cracked crystal. All just as Goldman had personally placed there not an hour before.

At the two-minute warning, a flurry of motion in the wings drew Goldman's attention. Across the set came a man almost as handsome as Hernan, with a smile that looked blinding in the stage lights. He extended his hand first to Kessler and then to Goldman himself.

"Gentlemen," he said. "Marty Hudson. You both ready for some fireworks?"

Goldman smiled, but Kessler's face remained a mask of rising anxiety. Goldman looked down at Kessler's hands, saw the fingers clenching and unclenching in his lap. *For once those hands won't be making any fireworks.* Goldman's smile widened.

"Ok, people, places."

Goldman recognized the voice of the production assistant from earlier in the green room. He squinted into the lights and finally got a look at her. Shoulder length blond hair. Breasts all but erupting from a blouse two sizes too small for her.

61

Wonder how she got this gig? Goldman thought as he heard her say, "Ready in five, four, three . . ."

She silently counted down the last two seconds on raised fingers, then pointed at Hudson as a red light came on one of the studio's two cameras.

"Good evening and welcome to this special live edition of *Exposed!* I'm your host Martin Hudson. Our two guests tonight need little introduction. For years, Gregor Kessler has mystified audiences and experts alike with amazing feats of apparent psychokinesis. His ability to locate water, start and stop watches and clocks and bend all types of metal objects with just his mind has earned him thousands of loyal followers—as well as more than a few skeptics."

As Hudson spoke, the overhead monitors filled with a video montage Goldman had seen many times before: early footage in Tel Aviv, a young Kessler astounding crowds on the street; a much later clip of Kessler in the White House, entertaining the President--the same montage currently being watched by hundreds of thousands (*millions? Be still, my heart!*) of viewers at home. Goldman merely glanced at the video, but found his gaze drawn by Kessler himself. The gleaming dark curls, a little gray now at the temples; olive skin; eyes like the smoke of distant fires. *A damned handsome man. Forgive me, Hernan.* But today, Kessler's eyes had a worried look and as the video concluded he cupped his chin between his thumb and forefinger, shaking his head almost imperceptibly.

Why? Goldman thought. *After all these years, why agree to this now?*

Hudson continued. "Probably the best known of these skeptics is my other guest tonight, James Goldman, who began his career as "The Great Goldman," a sleight-of-hand magician and escape artist whose own feats of endurance—including being encased in ice for 55 hours wearing nothing but swim trunks—earned him several world records. For the past decade, though, The Great Goldman has turned his attention to debunking those who claim supernatural powers—especially the claims of Gregor Kessler. Gentlemen, welcome."

"Thank you, Martin," Goldman said. Kessler remained silent.

"Mr. Goldman, let's begin with you. You yourself were once a magician's magician, a master illusionist. Why the sudden change of path? And why persist in what many would call a witch hunt against Mr. Kessler."

"No witch hunt," Goldman said, shaking his head adamantly. "That would imply he's a witch. Plainly and simply, the man is a fraud. I stopped creating illusions myself when I looked around at my audiences and realized that some of them believed—really *believed*—that I could do the things their eyes told them I could do. This man—"Goldman jabbed a finger in the air at Kessler, "—this man thrives on that same gullibility. He's built a career on it! He needs to be stopped, just like all charlatans."

Hudson turned to Kessler. "What say you, Mr. Kessler?"

Kessler took a long, steadying breath. "Mr. Goldman . . . I have heard Mr. Goldman's claims before. I only know the things I can do, the things all of you have seen me do, are real."

"Nonsense," Goldman interrupted. "Time and time again I have debunked all the familiar videos Mr. Kessler tries to pass off as actual feats of telekinesis. The pre-bent keys, the peeking through his fingers while he covers his eyes, the distractions and misdirection. And he hasn't answered one of my proofs— "

"Accusations," Kessler corrected, looking at Goldman for the first time.

Goldman smiled. "As you wish. He hasn't answered a single *accusation.* Until now. Quite frankly, I'm a little surprised he's agreed to this broadcast."

"Yes, Mr. Kessler," Hudson continued. "Why now? Why on *Exposed!"* Goldman thought he heard the sound of ratings gold in the way Hudson said the name of the show.

Kessler sighed. "I have nothing to hide. Nothing. I've just grown . . . tired of Mr. Goldman's antics and thought this might put an end to them once and for all."

"Fair enough," Hudson said. He turned his attention to the items on the table between them. "What can you tell us about these?"

"I'll tell you about them," Goldman said. "These are the items Mr. Kessler has claimed in the past he can manipulate with his mind. Spoons,

64

keys, broken watches. Several metal vials, some contain water, some don't. The only difference is these items were brought into the studio by my staff and have been under constant watch since they arrived. Mr. Kessler has had no previous access to them."

"Is this true, Mr. Kessler."

Kessler nodded, that look of distant worry still playing about his eyes.

"Well," Hudson said, "shall we begin the demonstration? What do you plan to do for us today?"

Kessler sighed and leaned forward in his chair. "Sometimes," he said, "*sometimes*, I can tell where there is water and where there is not."

A look of concentration sharpened his features, a look Goldman had seen and scoffed at hundreds of times. Only Goldman knew that all the vials contained not water but vodka: he and Hernan had filled them themselves after lunch as they sat chatting dreamily about the show and what was to follow.

"This is it, Papi," Hernan had said, filling one vial with vodka and then a shot glass which he raised in a toast. "Here's to The Great Goldman finally exposing Kessler as a fraud." He tossed back the shot and looked at Goldman, a filled shot glass untouched next to his glass of water. "Drink, Papi!"

"No," Goldman said, pushing the shot glass aside. "I have to keep my wits about me for the show. But you go on." He smiled at Hernan, at the way the vodka glistened seductively on his lower lip.

"Ok, I will." Hernan filled another vial then another shot which he raised between them. "To us, then."

Goldman's heart fluttered. Grinning, he touched his water glass to Hernan's. "Now *that* I will drink to. Mazel tov!"

To us, Goldman thought as the ice water chilled a path down his throat. What that meant today was more of a miracle than anything Gregor Kessler had ever claimed as one. For so long he'd had to keep his true self hidden, so long he'd begun to feel like his own skeleton in the closet from which he feared to emerge. Now, everything was changing so fast it made his head spin more than that one shot of vodka. Now he and Hernan could even be married, something he thought he'd never live to see. But it was happening tomorrow, after his triumph over Kessler. A small ceremony with a few close, loving friends in their apartment, then a quick cab ride to La Guardia and an overnight flight to Athens. By this time tomorrow, they'd be sipping ouzo in an infinity pool as blue as the Aegean that surrounded them--on their honeymoon.

Almost there, Goldman thought as he watched Kessler's hand hover over those very vials he and Hernan had toasted over earlier.

"Everything all right, Mr. Kessler?" Hudson asked.

Kessler shook his head. "I don't know. I'm not feeling strong today. Well, not today, but right here, right now. Not so strong."

"Are you saying you can't tell which ones contain water and which don't?"

66

Kessler sat back heavily in his chair. "I mean just what I said. I'm not strong. Not here, not now."

Despite the inevitability of the outcome, Goldman's heart began to pound. *I've got you, charlatan.* "Why don't you have him try a key? Or a spoon?"

"How about it, Mr. Kessler?"

Kessler's eyes met Goldman's and Goldman felt his breath catch in his throat. This close, the man was truly beautiful, his eyes like infinity pools themselves. Goldman felt the tug of eternity as he looked into Kessler's eyes, felt his own blood retreating from his cheeks, felt himself harden again in the sensual proximity of this doomed and beautiful man he'd set out to destroy.

"Very well," Kessler said. He picked up a spoon and held it loosely between his finger and thumb. He shook his head rejecting it, then tried another and another before finally tossing one down atop all the rest in a startling clatter. "No, none of them. They don't feel right."

Of course not, you poor beauty, Goldman thought with an unexpected twinge of remorse. *I put them all there myself. To trap you. To ruin you.*

"A key, perhaps?" Hudson urged.

Kessler sighed again, then chose the thickest and heaviest key on the table. He held it up in front of his eyes.

"You know," he said, "when I was a boy in Tel Aviv, I saw a film about the great Harry Houdini. About his illusions and escapes. And that's all I wanted: to escape. I thought if Houdini—his name was really Eric Weiss, you know? —if Houdini

67

could escape from his life into the world of magic and celebrity, then maybe why not Gregor Kessler, too?"

Goldman swallowed, forcing his eyes away from Kessler's eyes to the key. If he tried any deception with that key, Goldman would have him—despite his sudden misgivings.

"And I did for a while, you know? Came to America. Appeared on TV. I was even on the cover of *Time* magazine. But then came Mr. Goldman and all that seemed to end. Few believed in Gregor Kessler anymore, because The Great Goldman told them Kessler was a fraud."

Kessler rotated the key slowly in his fingers, but Goldman couldn't see any obvious trickery.

"I ran for a while, you know? Ducked his accusations. Refused to meet with him. But then I told myself, Houdini wouldn't have run. The Great Goldman himself wouldn't have run—even back when he was truly Great."

Goldman could feel Kessler's gaze on him, but he willed himself to keep his eyes on the key.

"So I told myself, no more running. People will believe what people believe. That has always been true, especially here in America. So here I am tonight. I'm not running anymore."

"What it sounds like you're saying," Hudson said, "is that Mr. Goldman is right. That you are a fraud."

"All I'm saying," Kessler said, "is that if people want to believe him, so be it." Kessler palmed the key and dropped his hand into his lap.

A few members of the studio audience began to clap, then a few more until soon they were applauding thunderously, so that Hudson had to quiet them to continue with the show.

"What say you to that, Mr. Goldman?" Hudson said. "Do you feel vindicated? Victorious?"

Goldman looked at Kessler's closed hand in his lap, felt his words coming out awkwardly. "I feel... why yes... I feel... good about this."

"Well there you have it, ladies and gentlemen," Hudson said, smiling electrically into the camera. Tonight, Gregor Kessler—*Exposed!*"

The audience erupted again in applause and the credits rolled on the monitors. The three men stood and Hudson shook their hands, first Kessler's then Goldman's. Goldman had turned to leave the stage, when he felt a hand at his elbow. Kessler, extending a hand.

"I'm tired," Kessler said. "I meant what I said. Tired of running. I haven't your endurance, old man."

Goldman looked into Kessler's face and felt the strongest compulsion to kiss this beautiful, defeated man, this fallen Dionysus. Instead, he took his hand.

Immediately a cold light seemed to fill Goldman's head and he felt something hard and metallic press into the palm. Kessler smiled a smile that Goldman seemed to feel in every molecule, first a heat then a penetrating chill that made him shiver visibly despite the heat from the studio lights. Then Kessler was pulling him close, still clasping his hand, his other hand pulling Goldman in by the shoulder. When they were close enough that their faces might touch, Kessler leaned closer and whispered in Goldman's ear.

"Enjoy your honeymoon. I hear the islands are beautiful this time of year."

Goldman's breath wouldn't come. That searing chill he'd felt at Kessler's touch seemed to have frozen his lungs, his chest and as he watched Kessler leave the studio, he actually wondered if he might be dying.

What's happening to me?

"Mr. Goldman?"

Goldman turned toward the voice close by on his right, eyes wide in panic.

"Mr. Goldman—are you all right?"

The production assistant. The one whose chief assets still threatened to burst out of her blouse, a smile fading, a look of concern spreading over her face.

Her *beautiful* face.

Suddenly Goldman could breathe again.

"I... fine...I'm f-fine."

"Oh, that's good," the young woman said, her face lighting up again in a smile. "I was a little worried there."

Look at those dimples, Goldman thought. *That Cupid's bow mouth.*

"I just wanted to say tonight's show was one of the best we've ever done," she said. "So dramatic. You were—well, you were awesome."

Goldman's gaze fell to the young woman's blouse, the breasts straining to get out. *I'd like to help with that*, he thought—

"Oh, Mr. Goldman!"

He heard her voice as if it were a thousand miles away. His knees turned to water, and he would have hit the ground if the production assistant hadn't dropped her clipboard and grabbed him. Goldman felt the heat of her body, smelled the shampoo on her hair and realized with a good deal of confusion that he was getting an erection.

A huge one.

"Papi!"

Hernan rushed out of the green room when he saw Goldman collapse, slipping his own arms around him, Hernan and the production assistant helping Goldman to a chair.

"Papi? Papi—you okay?"

"Wh--? Y-yes, I'm fine. Just a little light-headed."

"I'm sorry," the young woman said. "All of a sudden he just..."

"I know," Hernan said. "I saw. Thank you for your help."

She smiled a little sadly and laid her hand on the back of Goldman's. "Good luck to you both."

"Papi," Hernan said, "I'll get you some water.

Goldman nodded, but his attention was not on Hernan. He was watching that lovely young woman with the Cupid's bow mouth walk away, the way her jeans stretched tight over her ass. All the best parts of her body, it seemed, wanted out of those clothes.

What's happening to me? he thought again.

Then he noticed the sharp edge of something inside his fist. He opened his hand and saw what had once been a key was now twisted almost beyond recognition. The metal felt as feverishly warm as the blood pounding inside Goldman's veins.

"Here, Papi."

Goldman flinched as Hernan lay one hand on the back of his own, nearly knocking the water glass out of his hand.

"Easy, Papi. Drink."

Goldman took the glass in one trembling hand and raised it to his lips. In the other, he held the remains of Kessler's key, twisted now most improbably into the perfect shape of a heart.

***

The next day, the elated mood of their wedding guests felt palpable as Goldman and Hernan stood face-to-face before them in the garden of the house they had shared for years. The setting sun provided the perfect rose-colored light for the ceremony: two men who no longer needed to hide anything from anyone—two who were about to become one.

"Such a handsome couple," someone stage whispered. The others erupted into spontaneous applause.

"They make you blush, Papi."

Goldman saw Hernan smile and tried to return it. What he managed felt more like a grimace of pain. How could he tell Hernan he felt the garden spinning around him, that he wasn't blushing, that the pink in his face was the result of the terrified pounding of his heart?

"Do you have the rings?" the officiant asked.

Hernan reached into his pocket and produced the platinum band identical to the one in Goldman's pocket, the rings they had picked out together the moment the courts had said they could be wed. He slipped the ring onto Goldman's hand and repeated the officiant's words.

"Now you, Papi," Hernan whispered when Goldman seemed to hesitate.

Goldman reached into his pocket. When his fingers closed on Kessler's heart-key, he snatched his hand free as if he'd been bitten by something with fangs.

Light laughter spread among their guests.

"Papi," Hernan whispered. "Now is not the time for comedy."

No, Goldman thought, *there's nothing funny about this...*

***

A few flutes of champagne, a dozen or so air-kissed cheeks, Goldman and Hernan bid their guests farewell and climbed into a limo. Next stop, LaGuardia and from there, the Greek Isles.

On the plane, Hernan asked, "So, this is first class?" In his hand, a champagne flute much nicer than those at their wedding. Better vintage too.

"Hmm," Goldman replied.

"What's wrong, Papi? You haven't been yourself since we left the TV studio. This is a celebration. Your celebration. *Our* celebration."

73

Goldman wasn't listening. His attention was monopolized by the flight attendant up in the galley, the contours of her tight skirt, the perfect bob of her hair. And her neck. God, how he'd like to run his tongue over that neck.

He stifled a cry when Hernan cupped his growing erection under the thin blue airline blanket.

"That's more like it, Papi. But remember. Save it for Mykonos."

Hernan handed his glass to the flight attendant who smiled beautifully at him. As she turned back toward the galley, Hernan gave Goldman's cock a little squeeze.

Goldman's gorge rose at the feel of his husband's hand in his crotch. A long flight ahead. Then infinity pools. Egyptian cotton sheets in the honeymoon suite. And two men who had been joined as one, joining as one over and over again, till death do they part. He thought of Kessler's heart-shaped key and what Kessler had said in the TV studio before offering his hand before they touched.

I haven't your endurance, old man.

Endurance. Goldman felt a chill descend upon him as if he were a man encased in never-ending ice.

The Wall

Stuart Holland

Thursday was a strange day, a fatal one. I was standing at the wall when I sensed something was wrong. I should explain. The crowd around me, waving papers at those who were guiding them to the only entrance, were screaming urgently. The wall was twofold, a solid wall behind one made up of over a hundred soldiers who stood, a solid enough group, fingers on the triggers of their semi-automatic weapons, directing people forward, constantly watching the crowd. The soldier in front of me showed no sign of fear. He was a brave young man; I sensed that as soon as I looked in his eyes. Suddenly, behind me, I felt a commotion as someone pushed through to the line of soldiers, a young child held firmly in their hands, pleading with the nearest soldier to take the child to safety. Evidently the soldier was following orders and he did not react to the man's pleading. The man holding the child shouted ever more loudly, urgency in his voice. The child was crying, visibly disturbed. In her own language she cried,

"Please take me to safety, and save yourself," she pleaded with the emotionless soldier. Finally the crowd was moved on, just a few feet and I stood, once again, staring at the soldier. And then the feeling of death overwhelmed me.

"Oh no," I cried out silently.

"Oh my God, he has a bomb!" someone in the crowd shrieked/ I saw the man's coat open slightly. "He's going to blow us up."

The soldier looked into my face, suddenly realizing what was being shouted at him.

"Where?"

"Him," the voice in the crowd gesticulated in the direction of the man holding the young child. "Him," I repeated to myself.

And then it dawned on me, if he did trigger his suicide vest, hundreds of people were going to die, including those brave soldiers. Everyone was trapped.

I became vaguely aware of the soldier raising his gun and pointing it at the man.

"You, stop where you are or I fire!"

The man clearly heard the voice for he turned, losing his grip on the child's arm. The child began to run, but her escape was hampered by the thronging masses. As he turned to look in our direction I saw the evil smile on his face.

"Time to die," he said.

And then it all happened in a flash and a bang. I barely remember, but there was the sound of gunshot, then a loud bang. Instantly something red, jagged and fleshy shot past my head, followed by a rush of air and then smoke. I saw the soldiers in front of me fall to the ground, dead, their mutilated forms bleeding profusely. I sensed the panic and the death and then the pools of blood and flesh that fell on the ground around me. I looked up, glad that I had died of natural causes a few weeks earlier, glad my spirit could not be touched by all the carnage around me. And then, with the horror of what had just happened, I passed through the wall that lay behind the line of fallen soldiers and went to comfort those who had just been pulled from the carnage, those who were about to pass into my realm.

Repeat Performance

Dorothy Davies

Florabella hesitated in the church doorway, just as she had done a hundred times before. Count them, she thought, one hundred times. This is the one hundredth and first time and still there is no end to the coming here and the going through this and the going home again. I tire of it. I want it to end. It feels as if it will not end. It cannot end until penance is done. How many times, I wonder, does that entail?

She turned and smiled at her father for the one hundredth and first time and they began the slow walk down the aisle. Sunlight through the stained glass windows cast colours before her, petals to walk on, petals that would not catch her satin shoes and cause her to slip.

The church was full of flowers, in huge vases on pedestals, gathered into small bunches on the pew ends, trailed across the altar. Every year they were there, just as the wedding party was there. They too had become trapped in the never-ending cycle. Not a flower was different from the other one hundred times she had looked at them.

Florabella knew she was beautiful, knew the golden hair cascading down her back would catch the sunlight, just as the silks and satin of her wedding dress would reflect the sun in all its glory. She knew she was perfect, too perfect.

"You look lovely, darling." Her father's words, repeated every time at that moment, caused a pain to pierce her side and into her heart. She only looked good on that day at that time. She knew, as he did, that the other 364 days they lie mouldering under the great slabs in the Loverett chapel just over there, where the cameraman was hiding. At least he believed he was. Every year without fail for at least the last ten years he had tried to capture the wedding, every year he had gone home with a blank film. She gave him full marks for trying.

The guests turned as one at her entrance: Benjamin got to his feet and turned to look at her with open mouthed astonishment whilst his best man, Jeffrey, was as languid and indifferent to her as always. But then he preferred men, she knew that. Jeffrey was the cause of their problem, their endless repeating of the wedding. Jeffrey, the one who dabbled in the darkness, who called up demons and helped cast them, the entire wedding party, into this hell.

The vicar, an innocent trapped in their nightmare, stood waiting at the altar. He showed signs of strain, just as he always did. For him, as for all of them, the nightmare was the repetition. They were forced into an exact re-enactment with no chance of breaking the spell. Yet. She knew if she could find a way to make one tiny thing different, they would go to the spirit realms and carry on a life there. No waking on the 14th July and becoming their living selves again.

She caught a glimpse of utter repulsion in Jeffrey's eyes but saw the usual adoration in Benjamin's. He never seemed to grow tired of seeing his beloved walk toward him, of joining with her in marriage, of going in the landau back to the Loverett mansion and there –

There was the chance she had of changing the scenario. Not here, where the wedding went with military precision: hymns, prayers, exchanging of vows, exchanging of rings, the heavy scent of the flowers in her nostrils, the sight of her handsome husband in her eyes, the longing for the night in her loins, a night that never happened. She went to the altar - and her grave - a virgin.

Keep your film rolling, cameraman, she thought. It had taken her some time to find out who the person was and what he was trying to do – capture the yearly event on film to prove that ghosts existed. The idea amused her, as did making sure he never caught their images on the mechanical device. It was easy; they were wrapped around in invisibility to all but those with the gift of 'seeing' but film, no. He tried, tried hard but he would never succeed. And if I have my way, we won't be back next year, she thought with savage intent. Then what will he do for so-called 'ghost hunting?'

I need to walk away from the vestry after signing my name for the 101st time and say: *look, silly man, you are on a loser here. We are spirits trapped in a situation we cannot escape. We are not ghosts. In any event, they don't exist. What you think are ghosts are no more than people's lingering images caught in a time loop. Got it? We, on the other hand, are working out a penance for meddling or dabbling or messing with, choose your own descriptive word, with the dark side. That's all.*

But I can't do it, any more than I can change anything that happens when I go through this ceremony every year.

With Benjamin at my side, I walk back along the aisle, stepping on the colourful sunshine, smiling at each other, whilst I sense the glowering, menacing presence of Jeffrey right behind us. Each time we do this, each time we re-enact this ceremony, the menace grows stronger. I have to find a way to break this cycle!

Out into the sunshine and the well-wishers gathered outside, throwing rice at us, rice which catches in my hair and my bouquet. I shake it out; the birds need it more than I do.

The landau, also decorated with flowers, awaits us. Benjamin helps me to climb in and then sits down beside me, smiling with contentment and love. It is the best moment of all in this endlessly recycled day. From here on it just goes downhill fast.

"Florabella, I love you." Benjamin takes my hand, the one with its glittering new wedding ring, and kisses it. "I wish this moment could last forever."

"Hush," I tell him, as I do every time. "Be careful what you wish for, you just might get it."

He smiles. Poor darling doesn't understand the powerful thing thoughts and wishes are. Even after all this time.

Loverett Manor is a blaze of flowers and colour, a sumptuous feast awaits us, guests who did not come to the ceremony are standing around, glasses of punch in their hands and, for some, already in their bodies, judging by their red faces and extra loud conversations. We are greeted with congratulations, kisses and handshakes. It is a moment to treasure, especially when you know what is to come.

I sometimes ask myself at this point of the endlessly repeated day, how everyone could be so happy, smiling, confident and forward looking, when they know what is to come. But a thought occurs to me, for the first time, I have to admit. Do they know what is to come? Do we all know what we are doing, or am I the only person who knows that we are reliving this day as a penance for what is to come? I believe I am.

That is the first change, then. My thinking is different.

It is part way through the afternoon reception when it begins to go wrong. It is when Jeffrey has consumed enough punch or spirits of some kind to approach me as I am at the large open window looking out across the lawns at the trimmed hedges and flower beds. He stands by me, breathing alcoholic fumes into my neck. I am aware that despite his tendencies, he has some feeling for me, which has now been taken from him because of my marriage to his best friend.

"You stole Benjamin from me," he begins, as always.

"Benjamin was not yours to begin with."

"Ah, sweet Florabella, that's where you are wrong. Benjamin has always been mine. That which he will seek to put into you he has already put into me."

He seeks to shock me, as if I don't know what homosexual people do with one another to get satisfaction. Little does he know what I have overheard in my time. I am no innocent when it comes to sexual knowledge, only sexual experience.

"I will have him back!" he hisses, so low only I hear it. And that is when I know I have to act. I turn and throw a curse at him, one I have learned in the dark hours of training as a witch. He falls back, shocked, white faced and unsteady. He leans on a chair and the white slowly changes to a deep dark shocking red.

"Ah, the bride knows more than she lets on."

The hand gestures are something I don't know but the darkness he conjures is real. Guests begin to comment, to cry out, to utter oaths and make for the outside, but too late. The darkness smothers and covers and suddenly the very walls begin to bow outwards, the ceilings to sag towards us and the house – implodes.

No one escapes.

No one.

In the long lonely empty hours I spend in my coffin in my stone sarcophagus, I wonder how I did not realise Jeffrey had been meddling with the dark powers. I was so busy with my own white witch work to ensure I got the man I loved that I overlooked his work to ensure he kept the man he loved.

In the end we all lost, didn't we?

The Loverett chapel was full with so many of us needing to be buried that we were piled on top of one another in sturdy coffins meant to last a lifetime. I am above Benjamin, alongside my parents and a few relatives. I don't like it but at least I get out once a year to re-enact my wedding day, the proudest day of my life.

The cameraman would love to capture the occasion but what is important is the reason why we re-enact this wedding every year. If you meddle with any forces, white or black, there are repercussions. I used my powers wrongly, to try and injure someone. He used his powers wrongly and caused the death of a great many people. Between us, Jeffrey and I committed most of the cardinal sins – and we were condemned to pay the price. Until one or other of us breaks the pattern in some tiny, almost insignificant way, we will be doomed to relive this day forever. He has no intention of changing it. This I know, for he follows the pattern exactly where I hope to put a foot wrong and break it. I see his look, I know what it means. *You helped me create this; you are as doomed to do this as I am.* This I accept, only up to a point.

I hoped that my change of thinking would change the day this time. It wasn't enough.

I am back in my coffin, back in my dry as dust bones, my wedding dress stored for another twelve months. When the 14th July rolls around for the 102nd time, I will try again.

I wonder if the cameraman will be there next
time?

Made Of Stone

Paul Edwards

1.

"I baked a chocolate cake this morning," Sadie told the headstone, trying her best to smile. "We probably won't get round to eating it. I only baked it because it reminded me of you." Her smile vanished. "I know how much you used to love your chocolate cake. How you used to end up with it all round your mouth. It used to make us laugh so hard."

My gaze fixed itself to the ground.

There was only so much of this I could take.

Sadie would often express her frustration that I wouldn't talk. But we weren't really talking to Archie, were we?

The trees quietly rustled around us. The temperature was dropping. I couldn't interrupt her, not while she had more to say.

"I'm painting all the time," she said. "Usually portraits of you, my darling. Trying to imagine what you might have looked like now, based on the photographs and memories I have."

I didn't like looking at the photographs. Sadie could study them for hours. Sometimes I would have to come downstairs in the middle of the night and make her pack them all away.

"Well," trying to force another smile, "I suppose we'd better go." She nodded toward our house. "We're only over there, remember? And I carry you around with me everywhere. A part of you is with me now," she clasped a hand to her chest, "here; inside. And a part of me is with you, too." She pulled in a breath. "Wherever you are."

***

Later that evening, I noticed Sadie was reading a worn, dog-eared copy of *Frankenstein*.

She saw me looking.

"Did you know," she said, "that Mary Shelley had five pregnancies but only one surviving child?"

"It was common for children to die young those days."

"Her first child," Sadie said, undeterred by my air of general disinterest, "was a little girl named Clara. She died when she was just eight days old. Shelley wrote about a dream she had, where her child came back to life. It had only been cold, she wrote, and that when she rubbed it by the fire, it had lived again."

I closed my eyes. "Why don't you try and sleep?"

She sighed, then rolled away from me and switched off the lamp.

"There's so much pain in the world," she whispered at the darkness. "So much unavoidable, inescapable pain. No wonder people change, Nick. No wonder they become all twisted and bent out of shape. They don't mean to. It's just the pain and the hurt that turns them into monsters."

2.

"So," Lucy asked me, a couple of days later. "When are you going to tell her?"

We were sat together in Lucy's flat. As I contemplated a reply, I surveyed our surroundings. Lucy was an amateur photographer. There were photos pegged to lines stretching across the length of the room. She took lots of pictures of places around town and the way she caught them made them seem different and otherworldly. Maybe it was the camera she used, or the effect of the lighting perhaps. But she could make me see aspects of our town in new and arresting ways.

She laid her hand on my knee, giving it a squeeze. Her other hand drew her hair back away from her eyes. "It's plainly clear that you're only with her now out of sympathy," she said. "It's like you feel you're under some obligation, or duty, to stay. But the longer you leave it, the worse it's going to be."

I glanced at her again, remembering how she'd told me once that she loved me.

I saw her as a chance to begin again.

To become someone new.

She clasped her hands together, pushed them between her thighs. "You don't want to feel trapped like this. You know it's not right, Nick. You have to look after yourself. Put yourself first. Put *us* first.

And if she was being honest with herself, she'd accept it's over, too."

My gaze fixed on the many pictures on the wall of Lucy and I smiling and cosying up together. Looking happy. Content. That felt so unreal. Everywhere I looked, there was us in small square windows, frozen blissfully in time.

She saw me looking. "In this flat," she whispered, "between these walls, my world is all about you. But out there," she nodded toward the window, "we're separate. And I want the two to meet, Nick. I want that *so* much." Another sad smile. "I want to walk out there with you, my head held high. Not to be sneaking around behind people's backs like this. It's not fair on me. Not fair on her, either, really."

3.

The day I left Sadie will always stay with me; there are moments that will be painfully etched on my memory forever. I remember seeing Lucy first. It had been raining and she refused to let me enter her flat.

"I'm not going to wait for you forever," she said, leaning against the doorframe, watching me get colder and wetter out on the street. "I have a life too. The clock's ticking, mister. I'm not getting any younger."

"Lucy... *Please*. Just let me come in. We can talk about it inside. Not out here in the street."

"Not until you give me an answer." She folded her arms across her chest. "I've been waiting and

89

waiting. Carrying on but there's still no end in sight. What's it going to be, eh? Me or her?"

"I'll tell her," I said, nodding my head.

"Now?" she asked. "Will you tell her now?"

"Now."

And so that was exactly what happened; Lucy drove me to the house and I went in there and told Sadie everything.

It passed by in a blur. I've managed to successfully blank out most of the details. But I do remember the look in Sadie's eyes. The terrible, awful hurt.

I'd seen it before.

After Archie.

After everything we went through together.

I felt Archie's presence so keenly it was hard to speak. But I remained hard, cold and resolute.

And then I was gone, filled with so much shame and regret and much relief, too.

Lucy was waiting for me in her car.

I put my small bag of packed belongings in the footwell. Sat in the car beside her and closed the door.

She looked at me with her big, dark eyes.

"It's done," I said, and she smiled without saying a single word.

4.

Ironically, things never worked out between me and Lucy. She helped me to slip away, though, changing the direction my life was heading, but we quickly discovered that we didn't belong together.

I haven't seen her for months now. Think she might have even skipped town.

But I have been thinking lots about Sadie. I need to know she's okay. That she's surviving and she's well. I don't even know for sure that she's still living in our old house, the one right behind the cemetery.

I pass through the district where I used to live. An air of neglect has crept in. There are weeds and brambles everywhere. The streets seem so quiet. So still.

I make my way over to my old front door. Maybe she has someone new, I think. I genuinely hope so. I hope she's not alone. I draw in a breath, then knock. No reply. The door's ajar though, and I open it, slowly.

"Sadie?"

This place feels as cold and as still as a mausoleum. I slip inside, staring at all her pictures covering the walls. They appear to fill every patch of wall space – paintings of the house, the garden, us.

Always us.

Together.

As one.

I reach out, touching the three of us, briefly, hesitantly.

One painting depicts Archie as a handsome young man.

I know it's supposed to be him.

He has my colour eyes.

Her hair.

91

She is standing with him, arms wrapped around his waist. Her hair strangely raised and waving. Words in a balloon coming from her open mouth: *You are in my stone-cold heart.*

"Sadie?" I try again.

Just silence.

I head for the back door.

I think I know where she might be. Where she would go if she wasn't here.

The trees shake their bony fists at the heavens. Dead leaves swirl about my feet.

I see her up ahead, knelt on the earth in front of his headstone.

Of course she would be there. She is wearing her winter coat, I see, the hood pulled up. Surrounding us, black, hollow pairs of eyes catch my wandering gaze. The statues have built up and they appear so lonely, lost and sad. A sea of memorial statues, facing vacantly toward Sadie.

I stop behind her, steeling myself to speak.

"Hi."

She tilts her head just a fraction.

I still cannot see her face. In my head, I'm busy working out how long it's been. What, two years since I last saw her? Three?

"I knew you'd come back," she whispers.

"I came to see how you are," I say. "I needed to know you were okay. I'm sorry I..." I trail off.

The only sound for a moment is the dry rustling of the trees.

"*Here* is where we should be," she replies. "The three of us. Together. You can never imagine how badly I wanted that, Nick." A short pause. "Still do, in fact."

"I wanted it too," I say, but my voice sounds so small and faint, muffled by the rustling I hear. "But after everything we…"

"You don't know what you did," she says, straightening slowly.

I know now that I shouldn't have come. This is all just a bad mistake.

"Sadie…" I begin.

She starts turning her body toward me.

And I realise the rustling I hear isn't coming from the trees at all.

Carefully, she pulls back the hood of her coat.

The terrible hurt in her eyes has transformed into something else.

Something impossible.

"You want to see how I am?" she says, the rustling and hissing and slithering so very loud in my ears now.

Her wide eyes glow and I realise I won't be leaving this place ever again.

"Well," she says. "Look at me now."

Never Ending Litany

Diane Arrelle

We sat and stared at the surfboard. Short, brightly colored like a rainbow, that board was all we had left.

Bud had spent his entire life as a grasshopper, all play and no work and now as we sat at his memorial service, all he had to show for a lifetime of 35 short years was this piece of foam, fiberglass and epoxy resin.

I couldn't even cry. My eyes had cried too much and now they were dry. The only salt water left in my life was outside the old funeral home sitting on a shabby side street not far from the Atlantic Ocean. That ocean, oblivious to our grief, just kept pounding the sand over and over in a never-ending litany.

The service was short. There was little to say about my brother. He had been all I had left to love in the entire world and he had vanished into the surf while trying to catch just one more wave. *A fitting end*, I decided. *No, an inevitable end.*

The funeral director said in his soft, sympathetic voice, a voice trained to show compassion and ease pain even if it wasn't heartfelt, "And now, Bud's sister, Abigail, would like to say a few words."

I got up, still stiff from the long drive from the rolling mountains of Pennsylvania. I know it's normally a three-hour drive, but I took the four-hour route through farmlands and pine barrens, avoiding the AC Expressway filled with gamblers and late summer tourists. I walked slowly, took the few steps to the front, stood next to that surfboard and my mind went blank. *What would Bud want me to say*? I wondered and then I knew. He'd want me to say nothing. We never had to speak to communicate and I didn't have to speak now. "Thank you all for coming," I said to the small crowd of shore locals who were Bud's companions, not mine. Then I turned and left the building.

I walked down the street and looked for the places we'd hung out growing up. I passed the sprawling building replacing the old high school that stood for nearly a century. It made me nostalgic and sad. It had been a magnificent old castle, but progress had come to this tiny island city. Progress came in the shape of gambling palaces that destroyed all the real landmarks and filled the empty spaces with shiny, monstrous buildings covered in flashing, brightly colored lights, several of which now stood closed and dark.

Everything familiar was gone, the good with the bad. They razed the slums for luxury condos, they cleared the boardwalk of almost everything original. Between controlled detonations, mysterious fires and the demolition ball, the face of Atlantic City was forever altered. My memories were having a hard time competing with the present. Atlantic City had been my home for my first 21 years and through all the changes I knew that at least the sand and the ocean were still the same.

I turned and headed to the ramp leading up to the boardwalk. The weathered wooden slats hadn't been changed by progress and that was reassuring. I walked down the wooden ramp to the beach on the other side of the man-made dune and stared out at the gray expanse. The ocean was eternally the same, the waves rushing to shore, the waves pulling back to the depths only to roll back in and rush the shore again. It never ended, it never stopped, it just calmed down some days and roared with a vengeance on others.

I studied the ocean and thought about Bud. He had chosen to disappear forever on a vengeance day. He knew better than to surf in a storm ocean, he knew better than to surf after the sun set. I guess the call got too strong.

It had gotten too strong for me. I said I left to find work, I said I left because I had grown up too much for this island. But I knew that I really left because the call had become too strong and I was afraid to face it.

I felt a tear roll down my cheek. I was surprised I was still capable of crying and wondered if the tiny briny drop was for my lost brother, my lost youth, or for my cowardice.

The late September afternoon sun was shining, making the water glitter and sparkle in dancing patterns. I cocked my head and listened.

I heard it, the call but it was daytime faint. I knew the water was autumn warm and I started to head toward it. What harm would it do to wade out a little? The sun was out and I knew I'd be safe.

I headed onto the beach. The warm white sand gave beneath my feet and I felt like I was trudging through the desert. But as soon as I hit the high tide line, the sand became cool and hard and I burrowed my toes into the grayish surface. I was home and I felt that maybe, just maybe, all was not lost after all.

I took a step toward the water when the call became more intense. It was no longer tugging at me, it was pulling me in. I wanted to be afraid, but I knew the ocean loved me. I spent my entire life listening to it tell me so, with sub-verbal foreplay, sweet-talking me.

For the first time in 12 years I could feel its need and, as if no time had passed at all, I yielded to the sea. I stepped in up to my knees and let the water swirl around my legs, pulling, pulling gently, pulling back toward the deep and then shoving, gently shoving, back to the beach. Before I could help myself, I dove into a wave. I felt myself tumbling as the rough currents just under the surface grabbed me. I broke free, just like old times and stood in thigh deep water. I suddenly remembered that I had just been at my brother's memorial service when I realized that my black skirt was bunched up around my waist. I shrugged, smiled and dove in again. After all, the ocean was my home, no matter where I resided.

At one point I felt myself hit another swimmer. I had been riding a wave in when a thump broke my momentum. I tumbled head over heels then righted myself. I stood to see if the other swimmer was all right. There was no one there. I turned and searched

97

the shore, then the horizon, but I was alone. I shuddered, a ripple of fear going through me. I looked to the west, past the back bay and noticed that the sun was lower in the sky. It was late afternoon, time to head back to the hotel. I trudged out of the surf and, as I left the water, I shuddered again and not just from the late afternoon chill. Maybe after dinner, I'd visit Mom in the nursing home.

I didn't want to go there. She didn't know me, didn't know her son was gone. Harvey, the bastard, had shoved her out of their home on the island and made her live out her last years in limbo a few miles inland. I fought off the waves of sadness that threatened to overwhelm me. She never wanted to leave Absecon Island. It had always been her home, she was born here and deserved to die here.

Damn Harvey, anyway, I decided. He didn't deserve it, but he'd get their home---our home. I'm sure he made Mom signed it over to him before she got sick. If only Dad was alive, but that was the whole problem, Dad had drowned when I was 14 and Bud 16. Mom would say, "You can't expect me to live my entire life alone, can you?" every time one of us complained about her second husband, the rat bastard Harvey. I guess she was right. She deserved some happiness, after all, Dad died, not her. But Harvey... I never warmed to him.

I trudged through the powdery sand back to the boardwalk, seaweed in my hair and my clothing ruined by my little dip. The salt water was slowly drying on my skin and I was beginning to itch. The sand made my shoes rub. Gotta get back to the hotel, I decided when something grabbed my shoulder. My mind flashed back to my collision with no one in the water just a few minutes before and I screamed. The grip tightened. I pushed it off and spun around.

"Abby! I knew that was you!"

When I said there was no one back here for me, I was wrong. There was always Terry. I had spent years trying to forget Terry, yet here he was, grinning at me like I was the most exciting thing he had ever seen. "Abby, you look wonderful!"

I brushed at my hair hanging around my head in wet sandy clumps and struggled to push my skirt back down where it belonged. "Uh... Terry," I sputtered, totally unprepared for this meeting while remembering how I had secretly hoped for it. Only not quite like this. No, I had imagined myself a little more presentable and of course devastatingly beautiful because I like to pretend I had aged more than gracefully over the last decade.

I laughed.

He laughed. "God, it is so great to see you again. I... I think about you... a lot."

Before I could stop myself, I said, "I think about you too."

We shared a moment of awkward silence. *Guess it's the way it goes when love ends at an impasse*, I thought as I struggled to say something clever and noncommittal.

Terry broke the silence, "I went to the funeral home, but the service was over. That was quick."

"I'm sure Bud would have appreciated it."

"I didn't go for Bud. I went there to see you."

99

"Oh," was all I could manage. My eyes were burning and I realized that I had been wrong at that funeral home... there were still lots of tears left in me after all.

"I came up here and saw you coming out of the water. So I waited."

A cold fear rushed through me as I asked. "So who was the other swimmer I crashed into?"

Terry shrugged. "You were alone out there, fearless as always."

I shivered. Fearless may be the wrong word because I was suddenly feeling frightened by my inexplicable encounter out in the surf.

"Hey, you're cold. Why don't you go to your room and I'll come by in an hour or so and we can grab some dinner and talk... about old times."

"Ok," I agreed, "I'm staying two blocks down the boardwalk at a small beachfront place. You'll know which one." I giggled and he knew immediately which motel, the one we'd go to when either one of us had a couple of extra bucks. Then I gave him a quick peck on the cheek and rushed down the boardwalk, trying to work up some warmth in the chilled late afternoon/early evening air.

After I had gone to my room and changed, I stood on the second floor balcony and stared out at the dark gray waves playfully rushing toward the lighter gray beach. I glanced up and down the boardwalk looking for something familiar. Even this hotel, which was old and slightly dumpy, was surrounded by hotels both new and unfamiliar. I knew this block, I used to baby-sit at an old two story motel right down the way. I waitressed at the restaurant two blocks away, the restaurant now the site of a high-rise condo.

I was tired and didn't know what to do with myself for the next hour. In all the years I had lived here, I'd never cared for anyone except my family and Terry. I was a loner and now as I stood watching the daylight fade completely into night, I was totally alone.

The air got chillier or maybe it was the water getting darker. As much as I loved the ocean in the daytime, I feared it totally in the night. I didn't even know what drove me to take a room instead of driving back to the Poconos and the safety of the mountains.

Something lived in that ocean of darkness. Something a lot more than fish. I always felt it there and I always was afraid. I never joined in beach parties and I never made-out with the guys under the boardwalk. Everyone used to tell me I was nuts. I knew I wasn't.

Bud knew it too. And so did Mom, although she never admitted to it to me. But I knew. I'd overhear her warning Dad about night fishing. About the things that live in the waves. He always laughed at her. But she had been right. One night he went out and the next day he was found dead, washed up on the beach.

Whatever it was that lived inside the water, it hadn't wanted him. Dad had come from Chicago and never heard the call. All he ever heard was the crash of the waves.

Suddenly the call changed. It wasn't the call of the daytime ocean. No, it was the call of the night. The one I had to ignore. But it gave me an idea. I called and left a message for Terry. He never moved away or changed his number. I knew that because sometimes when I was particularly lonely, I'd call just to hear his recorded voice. I told him I had to go out, but if he wanted I could meet him later and left my cell number.

Then I drove to the nursing home to visit Mom. The nurse was nowhere to be seen so I entered without signing in. I went to Mom's room. She didn't know me, but that was to be expected. "Hi Mom, I've come to take you home. I've come to take you where you belong."

I got her on her feet and we marched right out of the building, no one was on duty to see us leave. I guess the nurse or orderly on duty decided to light up another smoke.

I put Mom in the passenger seat and drove back to the beach. She never said a word so I babbled just in case she could understand anything. I parked at my hotel and led Mom out to the slate colored beach. I could hear the waves and I could see that Mom was responding to them. She smiled.

I could hear the voice of the ocean clearly as well, but it wasn't calling to me. It was calling Mom. She smiled and nodded and stumbled toward the dark sea. The water was ebony, the sand a deep dark gray. The lights from the street above us didn't reach to the water.

"Mom, wait." I said and took her hand. "Is this what you want?

In answer, she pulled her hand from my grasp, gently ran her fingers along my face and then turned her back to me and walked into the dark abyss of the ocean. I lost sight of her almost immediately. It looked as if she stumbled but at the same time, I swear she looked as if she were being pulled down under the waves.

I waited, the voice became voices, the call became stronger. I wanted to turn and run away, I wanted to rush into the water and save my mother. Instead, I just stood and finally let all the pent up tears fall. "MOM!"

She never came up again. She was gone. "Mom," I called, "Mom, are you with Bud? I love you!"

I stood for another half hour or so, then backed away. The calling had stopped. No one wanted me any more tonight. I caught a feeling coming from the surf, from inside the waves. I swear I felt love.

I sat on the steps leading to the boardwalk and wondered if I were some kind of monster. I had just killed my mother and all I could feel was love and contentment. I knew she was happy now, at peace. Harvey would get the house, I could go home after her memorial service, after all, there'd be nobody and no reason to ever return. Mom was where she wanted to be, in the place she had always loved.

Someone touched my shoulder. Without thinking I tried to pull away and screamed. Either the police had found me out or the things under the water were going to finally get me.

"Hey, Abby," Terry said. "I thought that was you. Boy, are you jumpy."

I turned to face him and grabbed hold of him. He was warm and alive and felt just as good as he had all those years ago. He wrapped his arms around me and we stood there. I wanted to tell him about Mom, to blurt out that I had let her die, that I had caused her to die. I kissed him instead.

We went back to my room and took up where we had left off, in mid-affair. I slept beside him wrapped in his arms and wondered why I had ever insisted on leaving this place. I loved Atlantic City and so did he. He understood the ocean and its voices and he was strong enough to withstand them. I knew I could never have that strength, so I ran. I ran away from the only man I had ever and would ever love, I ran away from my family. I had been a coward. Bud had been the brave one. He knew his fate and had stayed to meet it. Well, I was back now and if Terry wanted me too, I would stay to meet my fate as well, whatever it was to be.

The next morning Harvey called my room. Even if he didn't come to the service, he'd been aware that I was in town. "Hello, Abigail, your mother wandered away from the home. Obviously the security wasn't very good there. The police are looking for her now. I'll call you when I hear something."

He hung up. He hadn't waited for me to speak; he just said what he had to say and hung up.

Just as well, I decided. No one was going to find her, I knew she was gone and wouldn't wash up later. Bud would never wash up and neither would Mom. The sea had called them and the sea would keep them. I turned to see Terry watching me.

"Hi there," I said and tried to purr. He reached for me and we spent the entire day in bed, eating chips and drinking soda from the vending machines.

When the sun began to set, he rose, took a shower and announced, "I want to take you out to that dinner we missed last night. Get dressed."

I obeyed and we went out to one our favorite restaurants for dinner. We ate at a wonderfully cheap but satisfying hole in the wall where we had shared so many meals in the past. Then we walked on the almost deserted boardwalk. A fog was rolling in and he said, "I want to make love to you on the beach."

The voice that rolled in with the surf told me that that was a great idea. "NO!"

"Why not? Are you still afraid the beach at night?"

"You know I am."

"Just come down, you will see, it's safe. I walk the beach all the time at night."

"Don't the voices talk to you? Don't they tell you to join them?"

"I decided a long time ago that the voices weren't real, it is just the sounds of the waves meeting the shore."

"The voices are real and now more voices have joined in. Can't you hear what they say?"

He laughed a kind gentle laugh. "What do they tell you, Abby? Do they tell you that you are beautiful and that I love you?"

"They tell me that they love me," I whispered. "They want to love me forever."

He took my hand and pulled me down onto the sandy beach. "Come with me, I'm strong enough to protect you from whatever you think is out there. Let me show you that there is nothing to be afraid of in the water."

"I can't!" I tried to pull away. "I'm afraid. What if they finally get me?"

He pulled me along and soon we stood at the water's edge. We stood in silence for a moment and the voices stopped. "See?" Terry said. "Nothing to fear."

I looked at him but it was too dark to see his face. "You heard them and you heard them stop." I said with a gasp. "You do hear them!"

"Sometimes," he said. "But I've gone swimming with them and they never hurt me. They don't want me and I'll make sure they don't want you. You are mine now. Come wade out a bit and I'll protect you."

I let him lead me out into the black water, into the place that scared me the most. The air was chilly and the water warm. It felt good brushing and swirling around my legs and then my thighs. It got higher and I felt safe holding onto Terry's warm secure hand.

I began to relax and let the fear go when the voices bellowed to me. They called me by name and, before I could react, a wave smashed into me

106

and knocked me off my feet. I lost my grip on Terry's hand as the voices called, "Abigail, we've waited. You belong to us, you belong here with us. We love you Abigail. Stay!"

"No," I screamed. The water rushed into my mouth and down my throat. I struggled to find Terry's hand and bumped into him. I grabbed his legs and tried to pull myself up. Something from inside the waves grabbed me, held me down. The legs weren't Terry at all. They were from something inside the waves. I opened my mouth to scream again and the salt water washed into my lungs. I felt this incredible rush of sadness and loss as I breathed in the briny death. I was never going to be with Terry. I was going to die. I'd never wash to shore, just like Mom, Bud and all the other drowning victims who disappeared forever. I was doomed to die just as I'd finally accepted happiness.

I wondered why I was still under the waves, still alive. I had stopped breathing and I was losing myself, my form. I was changing, melting, melding, becoming the ocean and yet still separate. I looked around and could see with a new vision. I was surrounded by others like me, formless yet still there.

"Welcome, Abigail, the voices inside the waves said. "You made us wait a long time for you to come home."

"I don't understand," I said, but then I did. Some souls just belong to another place, souls like mine I realized. And like Bud and like Mom, who were both there with me. I wasn't dead, I was just changed. I had joined my real family, the ones who would love me forever. We were in the place we belonged.

I looked out through the cresting wave that surrounded me and I could see the lights of Atlantic City, shining across the beach. "It's pretty," I said and the voices agreed.

"It will always be pretty in one form or another and we will always be here to see it."

I felt a rush of remorse as I saw Terry standing at the water's edge, screaming my name. "Poor Terry," I sighed. "I loved him."

"Don't regret, Abigail. He hears us as a voice. When you join us it will become voices and our voices combined are strong. Call to him and he will join you, he can hear and he is meant to be with us. Be patient and you will be together forever. We are the never ending litany."

the next wave crested around me and I saw Terry fall to his knees and sob.

"I love you," I said and he looked up.

I knew everything would be all right someday, because he had heard my voice in the waves.

108

Hag Stone

S J Townend

Reece pushed aside the cobweb strings on the photograph. *So this was her.* Aello.

It seemed Aello, his grandmother, had worn her black hair long in youth too, but had not cared to dye or mask the clean white streak like his mother had with hers.

Cropped and ashen was how his mother wore her locks now and his grandmother, she was all ash too, scattered in the forest near her home. Reece had not attended the old lady's funeral. He'd never even met Aello—his mother had ensured all her matriarchal connections were severed.

The rye bloomer baking in the oven drew him back to the kitchen. From Aello's cupboards, he fumbled together a picnic to accompany the loaf. A few comestibles had not been claimed by mould: a jam of sorts, dried fruit, preserved sausage meat from the larder.

The boat out front, tethered to an oak, was still watertight and so, after a hard day of boxing trinkets, burning musky, stained robes and pouring unidentifiable concoctions the old bag had been stewing down the sink, he'd decided he would venture out in it. The liberty of the vessel had beckoned him and the river had called out to the boat.

There was nothing of entertainment inside the cottage anyhow; no wi-fi or phone signal and nothing to read bar a few dust-coated novels he'd found the night before by the fireplace. They were written in a language he couldn't identify, filled with vintage copperplate engraving prints of ships, sea monsters heralding tridents and bird-like creatures with the faces of women and all more odorous than his grandmother's deathbed.

"Don't call us, we'll call you," he'd said as he'd tossed the books onto the fire.

***

When the probate letter came, stating that everything Aello owned was to be passed to Reece's mother, Reece suggested he went to manage the property. He met his mother in a motorway cafe midway between their homes. They rarely spoke—she wasn't one for talking and he wasn't one for listening. She told him she didn't want anything to do with the handling of Aello's estate and Reece, sensing his mother's hesitance to handle the situation, smelled cash.

"I'll go. For fifty per cent of the equity when the sale goes through."

"Okay. You go. Empty the place. Give away or bin or burn her belongings. Don't bring anything back for me, I want no memories saved." He watched his mother's eyes dampen.

"Seventy-five."

His mother wiped a tear and tilted her head to the side.

"I'll take seventy-five percent of the profit—as I'm doing all the work."

"Fine. I imagine it'll take you some time to clear it out." She paused. "The forest. Don't go into it, Reece."

His mother reached out and squeezed his arm gently, in a vain attempt to reinforce her words. She knew her son rarely did as he was asked and usually did quite the opposite. One could only lead the horse as far as the water.

"If you do though, if you really need to get out of the house for a break, please don't go any further than Phineas Island."

"Phineas what? How can there be an island there? She lives twenty miles inland."

"It's a riverine island—where the river splits and rejoins. Two miles south of the cottage. Tangled mangroves. Nothing good ever happened there."

Reece guffawed and rolled his eyes. "Christ alive, Mum. I'm not a kid. I'm not going to get lost in the woods, or paddle out of my depth, or follow strangers back into houses made of candy canes."

Reece's mother forced a smile at her son but, burnt by his sarcasm, she drew her hand away and looked down at her food. Her face twisted from concern to disgust as with delicate finger tips, she withdrew and flicked away a small, blue-black feather from her half-eaten gateaux.

***

111

When Reece woke up, he found he was in a hole; a cave of sorts, dark as a lonely midnight. He pulled his hand up to his head. He hadn't hit it. There was no blood, nothing that felt tepid and moist to touch.

His back hurt. He reached over, feeling between his shoulder blades, finding warmth and dampness. He winced as his fingers probed for a reason. Through his skin-thin t-shirt, his fingertips fell into deep, fresh lacerations. Something had dug in deeply. Blood soaked through his clothing. He could smell the metal of it, warmed copper.

His palms and knees also felt grazed raw, as if he'd dropped from a substantial height and then crawled on all fours through a thicket of needles and scouring pads.

He put his picnic sack aboard, set the boat to water, sat down on the wooden seat it offered—these are the things he recalled. The wind had picked up, enough so to feel skin on his hands and cheeks rippling. A gale had carried him onwards, forwards, down the river and away from the old hag's house, leaving the oar redundant. After this, he could recall nothing.

Had he blown into this pit? Tripped? Had he been drugged and mugged? He wasn't wet, so he can't have capsized. And where was the boat? His bag?

He stood, rubbed his eyes and brushed leaf litter from his limbs. A look up and side to side showed the same: nothing. Darkness. His body ached like never before, as if he'd fallen asleep in a tumble drier, hurled and spun and wrung inside its drum and burnt with detergent powder; as if yanked

112

out and pegged to the line with the force of a million winds slapping his face and body as he dried.

He turned to look behind him. The place was as dark as a badger's set and smelled as bad as fox shit. Behind him was a small wooden table and on it were just three things. Panic shook hands with his pain.

Reece knelt by the table, the ground beneath him damp, sticky. Had he knelt in some kind of mucilaginous exudate? Vomit rose high in his throat. Blindly, he fumbled for something, anything, to clear off the adhesive residue and settled on a handful of crisp leaves to wipe his wet knees clean.

The first object on the table was an oil lamp, which yielded him a radius of light no larger than a fistful of bad dreams, at the ends of which sat blackness again and the unknown once more. He reached for the handle at the top of the lamp and drew it along the table top, towards the other objects, so he could inspect them more closely.

The second item was a large pebble placed on top of the third item, a note of sorts.

The rock appeared to be used as a paperweight, despite the air in the cave being as quiescent and thick as a mug of solidified dripping. Reece held the pebble close to the lamp—it was smooth and grey with a thin sandwich filling stripe of white streaking through its mass.

He held it in his hand. It filled his hand. In such a claustrophobic place of darkness, to hold onto something so solid felt like stumbling upon an old friend, alive, amidst a warzone.

The rock had a hole that started on one side and went right through to the other, cleanly so, with the diameter the size of a fat finger. He slipped it onto his forefinger like a Paleolithic wedding ring, like a metamorphic bagel. He pocketed the rock and kept his hand on it as he moved the final item, the note, toward the dim light. The weight of the pebble gave him comfort, a peculiar reassurance, his finger fell in love with the hole.

The final item was the note which was tarnished around the edges—perhaps with time, perhaps with touch—and on it was just one sentence:

DO NOT LOOK THROUGH THE HOLE IN THE STONE,
OR YOU WILL GO THROUGH IT.

The words curled out of his lips in silence and again with sound blown into them. He shouted the sentence a third time and kicked the table with force. The table shot across the floor, crashing against a wall which he could not see as the words bounced back and forth in his mind, oscillating like a spring dangling between sanity and the alternative. How could he look through the damn hole in the stone even if he wanted to, when he could see no further than an inch in front of his nose?

***

114

With time, the cavernous silence became deafening. The words on the note had at first shouted at Reece, but then faded into insignificance as desolation bit back. The soundlessness, as haunting as the darkness, was broken only by his heart thrumming against the prison cage bars of his chest and his impatient feet snapping twigs on the floor.

Tired and crying, he slumped against cold granite. He put the lamp between his legs in an attempt to rest, then stood up again as the silence was interrupted by a flicking sound. A snake whipped across the floor toward him. In defence, he found himself lifting his foot up and down, stamping and screaming as the reptile's guts splayed across the sticks and leaf and mangled feather litter that made the dank chamber carpet. His shriek echoed, ricocheting upward, until it went, off with the soul of the snake, up, up, to somewhere Reece may never find.

He reached into his pocket and found the stone with the hole and ran his finger around and through it, around and around and through it again, finding once more a strange comfort in the regularity, the coldness of it, its hardness and the fact that it had an in and an out to it—somewhere his finger could enter and then leave.

He began to circle the dungeon floor, the edge of his foot pressing, dragging against the edge of the pit. He paced the circumference around and around and around again as the words on the note span and jostled between his ears, bubbling over in his cauldron of madness. All the while, he searched for meaning and for a gap in the jagged, rough rock wall through which he could escape. He grappled at the wall and floor of the pit with his hands, bringing the dim light of the lamp to each square inch, looking for help, a way out—seeking anything other than darkness, twigs, stinking feathers, cold, old rock and patches of slimy mud.

His body ached. His clarity started to crack. The light from the lamp, like his adrenaline-fuelled energy, simmered down and out. It became as dark as death. Reece fell asleep with five sore, bleeding, muddied fingers wrapped around a broken table leg and five fingers around the pebble in his pocket.

***

He woke. A circle of warm light hung around something on the twig carpet—his picnic. Reece, bitter at finding himself still trapped in such fresh hell, yet ravenous, parched, crawled over to the circle of illumination and reached for his food. He pulled his hand back in disgust. The bread and meat he'd wrapped just yesterday lay riddled, throbbing with dancing maggots, covered in spores and blue-green mould. His stomach flipped. Dry wretches of vomit erupted onto the pile of rotten spoils.

He wiped his mouth and noticed: as disgusting as the pile was, in it, he had seen. Light. Colour. Where was this light coming from? He looked up to see another circle of light, this one azure blue and laced with white clouds and laughing at his misfortune, boasting of a better place. And now, with the sliver of light the hole let in, he saw a rope ladder had been unfurled, leading up and out of the pit.

Reece stood, transfixed for a moment. He looked through the hole in the stone ceiling of the cave, a prisoner of granite and nightmares and released a guttural scream. This was followed by his own insane laughter. He climbed up.

He had looked up and out through the hole in the stone cave and yes, yes, yes, fuck, yes again, he wanted to go through it and go through it he would and he did. Screw the fucking note.

Someone was playing games with him, but he had beaten them. No-one told Reece what to do. No-one. He could see the fucking hole. He looked through and out of the hole to way up above at the beckoning blue sky and then he went out through it.

***

Reece hauled himself out of the top. In the light of day, his white t-shirt was red and brown with blood and dirt and his legs were covered in bruises. In front of him he saw his boat, moored, with his bag inside, which still contained his phone, wallet and keys.

He stretched out the crook in his back and felt something hard in his pocket.

The stone.

He drew it out. It had felt so smooth and comforting in the night, a salvaged piece of beauty amongst the hellish void of the pit behind him but under the radiance of the sunshine, surrounded by the beauty and the colour of freedom and the forest, all Reece saw was a dull pebble with a hole.

He marvelled at the ring of blue above his head where the forest canopy broke, letting the bright beams of light through. He inhaled the greens of the foliage. He held the lacklustre pebble up so that the hole haloed the sun, he looked at it in search of the beauty he was sure it had held in the black of night in the pit. He tried to see if the pebble had anything further to offer. Was it worth keeping as a keepsake? Should he lob it into the woods? He drew it closer to his eye, to inspect it further, to inspect it for patterns, to search for evidence of quartz or fossils.

Zilch.

Nada.

He lifted the central tunnel, the hole in its core, up close to his face. He pressed the stone on his cheek and brow, made a monocle of it for his right eye. He opened his right eye, whilst closing his left and looked straight through the hole... and saw, for a second... straight out the other side.

Before he had finished his sigh of disappointment, the piece of smoothed rock clamped hard against his face, no longer feeling fresh and cool, but burning hot like molten lava.

He screamed louder than he had ever screamed before as he tried to pull the pebble from his face, yet it clamped like the suckers of a hundred giant squid. A pressure built up in his eyeball as the pebble slurped tighter still. Pain pinballed inside of his head.

What was this satanic fellatio his face was being given?

His white eyeball reddened as the vessels burst, spilling blood into the socket. Blood squirted out with vitreous humour as his eyeball popped outright like a pus-filled miniature balloon. Gelatinous contents were guzzled in and through the hole and out the other side, spraying all over the forest floor. Nose and cheeks followed, sucked through the tunnel like light into a black hole. Flesh ripped from bone, claret poured down his neck as the rest of his face threaded through, becoming shredded, pulped like chunks of meat down a waste disposal system. Forehead and ears became ground up into a jammy mess, before being sprayed out of the other side of the rock.

Reece was running around in circles like a headless chicken, with just a gash for a mouth left to scream through, a rock clamped firmly to his neck stump, chomping, sucking and peeling back adipose tissue, feasting on cartilage and bone, mangling it through its granite mouth. His lips— two plump juicy red slugs—were torn off and swilled through, then the bones, muscles and fat in his neck became mushed and twisted and chopped like pulled pork and were churned out of the other side.

Like chemical fertiliser from the devil's crop sprayer, a zoetrope of red and pink and shards of grated bone spewed out onto the forest floor through the hole.

Torso, arms and legs followed. His testicles popped like overripe kiwi as they were ratcheted up close to the deadly portal, spraying semen through and out of the hole, a bukkaki party of one. Macerated, liquefied, dead, in and through and out of the hole, Reece became a puddle—reverse-birthed. A pool of cells and red slosh on the other side of the hole, his body fed the river.

The stone with a hole fell to the floor with a thud and all the birds in the trees cawed, "Aello Aello," and took to the air at once.

A colossal raptor with feathered wings, beetle-black eyes, long dark hair with a magpie's mallen, and baring the face of a woman cawed the loudest. The she-beast swooped down from the highest branch, retrieved the resting stone with the hole in from its mossy spot and dropped it down, back into the pit.

Held to Account

Michael B Fletcher

The scream bubbling in my throat, the stale air rushing to give voice to my panic and the pain of my bleeding fingertips all served to tell me I wasn't dead. My death should have been easier.

And I deserved it.

Who but I could be the one to do this? It was my fault, my reasoning that we were in such a parlous situation and consequently it was my life on the line. I had given an undertaking to my people that I would make the sacrifice, take the blame and a King's word is his bond.

So why was I still alive instead of meeting the Gods? Why wasn't I dead? Why was I engaging in a pitiful, self-serving scrabble for life?

The scream gave voice, a bellow blasting my eardrums in the enclosed space. Once only, for as I tried to draw breath for a second yell, my air ran out.

I drove bloodied fingers into the hard wood above my head, once, twice, but nothing gave. I was going to die but fighting for my life, like a coward. I attempted to withdraw into my mind, make my transition as easy as possible, but I didn't have the courage to do this. My next breath would be my last and I would be left with my struggles etched upon my face for all eternity.

Foul air trickled into my lungs as I fought against meeting the Gods.

A hiss broke through my stupor, encouraging me to take a breath. Sweet air flowed into my lungs and, like a drowning man saved from the cruel sea, I grabbed at the prospect of life and took it with both hands. A burst of light flooded my eyes as the coffin lid opened and I looked up.

'By the Gods, he's not dead!' exclaimed a male voice.

I welcomed the voice, not the words.

'Take me out! Now!' I screamed as I tried to rise.

'Oh no, your Highness,' he said, his hands pushing firmly on my shoulders, 'that we cannot do. You must die again.'

'No!'

'The Gods are not appeased. The fault is found. The system will not fail again.'

'No!' I pushed at the descending lid. 'I'm reprieved. The Gods don't want me. Let me live!' The lid slammed shut and the hiss of gas began. Not the sweetness of oxygen this time but the smell of bitter almonds.

I was foolish to think I would be granted this chance of a second life - I hadn't finished paying for the first.

In Sickness

Travis Mushanski

"Just shut up and drive," Patrick growled from the passenger seat. The gun quivered in his hand, but its muzzle stayed trained on the man in the driver seat. His shallow breathing was rapid and made a wheezing hiss as he breathed in.

"Okay! Okay! Cool, man," Joss managed to mumble. "Just asking where we're going." Sweat beaded down the back of his neck. He clenched the steering wheel to control the muscle spasms fluttering through his chest.

"Just shut up and follow the GPS. We'll get there when we get there." Patrick rubbed his temples as the ringing migraine began to sweep through his vision. "I just need to think!"

The anxiety was eating its way through Patrick's system and he wasn't sure what would happen when he reached breaking point. With one hand, he pulled out a cigarette, lit it and took a long drag. He cracked the window of the Lexus as bluish cigarette smoke wormed its way from his lungs in a tight, churning cyclone that vacuumed out the window. Neon signs blurred past the car as it sped its way through the downtown core. A red light burst to life in front of them, and Joss slammed the car to an abrupt stop.

Patrick could see Joss' eyes dart from one side of the intersection to the other. Cars spilled into the intersection oblivious to the situation playing itself

123

out in their confined space of the Lexus. "Don't do anything stupid," Patrick warned Joss. He cocked the pistol and shifted in his seat to block its sight as pedestrians passed.

Joss fidgeted in his seat and gave a quick nod. His knuckles were white from gripping the wheel too tight. He gave his right hand a shake to free himself from the agony of pins and needles, then scratched the side of his head and went back to the steering wheel. He scanned the cold steel revolver with his peripherals. Violent images shuffled through his mind. Explosions of blood and gore he had seen in movies. Messy. But in reality, a bullet moving miles per second could be as surgical as a scalpel. Despite the desperation growing inside of him, he accelerated through the intersection as the light turned green.

"Think I could have one of those smokes?" Joss asked meekly. Patrick shrugged and lit him a cigarette with the remaining nub of a smoke dangling from his lips. Patrick didn't say a word as he handed him the cigarette. Joss masked his gaze from Patrick's cold sunken eyes and shakily took the cigarette. The burning tobacco smoke saturated his lungs and the nicotine ravaged through his system. With an audible sigh, Joss loosened his grip on the steering wheel and sunk back into the Lexus' driver seat.

It was when Joss eased the vehicle into a residential area that he had noticed a sticky glean reflecting off a substance on Patrick's hand. It glowed an eerie crimson beneath the fiery orange streetlights. "Is your arm bleeding?" Joss broke the

124

long-standing silence. Until that moment, the quiet had only been broken by the car navigation system's cold monotone voice. The dread, confusion and concern in Joss' voice was startling, even to himself.

"Ah, fuck," Patrick said as he held up his gun arm. A trail of gelatinous blood had streamed its way across the back of his hand and began to pool on his leg.

"Need me to pull over?" Joss kept driving, but out of the corner of his eye, he watched as Patrick began to panic.

"No. Keep driving." Patrick carelessly tossed the pistol onto the dashboard and began to peel off his suit jacket. Underneath, the arm of his dress shirt was soaked with a mixture of curdling blood and mint-green pus. It throbbed and pulsed. As if triggered by sight, the pain suddenly rippled across his nervous system, causing Patrick to double over. He dry-heaved violently between his knees, filling the vehicle with the stench of bile mingled with a nauseating funk emanating from the necrotic wound.

"Holly fuck, dude!" Joss struggled to keep control of the car. "Fuck this. I'm taking you to the hospital."

Patrick snatched the gun off the dashboard and, with spit dripping off his chin, said, "Change course and I blow your fucking head off, asshole!" Patrick stared down the barrel of the gun and smiled as Joss' eyes widened with shock. The car suddenly swerved into oncoming traffic, but Joss instinctively pulled back into his own lane. The force of the sudden movement caused Patrick's head to smash into passenger side window.

"Jesus, shit, man!" Patrick roared. Blood trickled down the side of his forehead. "We're almost there now, just hold your shit together." He awkwardly unbuttoned his dress shirt. "Just have to get home and we're good." He twisted in his seat and stripped off the shirt, making sure not to loosen the grip on the pistol.

The pain was overwhelming, but the sight of it made a wave of nausea wash over him. Flesh on the perimeter of the wound was noticeably dying and turning a deep shade of purple- black. He fought the urge to pass out and wrapped the dress shirt tightly around the festering wound. His stomach churned as he felt the green pus became mashed beneath the pressure of the tightened tourniquet. It was the black veins running out from the center wound that spoke gravely for his condition. He was suddenly aware of the brief time he had remaining.

By the time Joss parked the Lexus in front of a moderate sized bungalow, a fever had spread unchecked through Patrick's body. He wheezed painfully but stubbornly hung on to consciousness. Long black tendrils weaved their way up his arm coursed their way across his chest. He pulled himself up straight from his hunched position and wiped off the long strings of yellow drool dangling from his chin. He twisted his neck unnaturally to each side. breaking the silence with a violent crack of bone. He tilted his head to Joss, smiled a rotten brown smile and gestured with a flick of the revolver for him to exit the vehicle

"I'm done. If you're gonna shoot me, just do it already!" Joss shouted at Patrick and crossed his arms in defiance.

Without warning, the steering column of the Lexus exploded into bits of plastic and electrical components, a hole was blasted through the windshield, causing a violent wave to implode shards of broken glass and Joss' right elbow condensed into a brilliant crimson mist. Both the men's skulls were ripped apart by a soul shattering screech caused by the close proximity of the gun blasts. Neither could hear the vehicle's panic alarm blaring into the night sky.

Joss had been too fixated by the jets of blood spurting out of the stump of his right arm to notice the driver side door swing open. To watch your own life force being pulled out of your body by an invisible force was truly a magical thing. Shock had torn him out of his own body to become a spectator in the last moments of his life. The pain had been replaced by a dull numbness caused by his circulatory system running out of blood. He hadn't felt the light tug on his shirt, but his body responded trance-like to Patrick's touch as he was led into the ominous house at gunpoint.

Joss watched in horror as his body was prodded down a desolate dark hallway lit only by the light escaping an open door at the far end. While his body refused to obey any of his commands, he was still being fed sensory data from his dying brain. The scent of lemon bleach hung heavy in the air, but as they neared the back room, he realized what the bleach was failing to cover up. The foul aroma of rotting flesh was so intense that it burned his nostrils. His senses were overwhelmed to the point that he swore he could actually taste the putrefied flesh of a long dead animal.

A pitiful moan echoed through the hallway, causing the two men to freeze in their tracks. A clunk of heavy chain signaled Patrick to press the revolver into the small of Joss' back, forcing him towards the room that bled light into the hallway. The moaning grew into growls and gurgling as the two men neared the door. Unnatural shadows spilled into the hallway making grotesque shapes that did not resemble anything found in nature. They clawed out at the men whose own shadows shrunk back in response, yet despite the ghastly figures, Patrick pushed onward, forcing Joss' body into the room.

The abomination before him was too much for Joss to comprehend. From some force beyond space and time, his spectral form was forced to witness the corruption of all that is natural and good in the world. The creature thrashed violently about the bed, soaked in visceral gore and bodily fluids. The creature's body was little more than rot and decay covered bones that had splattered pus, black ichor, and grey sludge throughout the room. It took no notice of the men as they walked across the threshold into its den; rather, it focused on tearing and clawing at the heavy cask-iron collar wrapped around its neck. Its growls and gurgling moans did little to convince the thick chain to free it from its imprisonment.

"My love," Patrick lovingly called out to the grotesque ghoul on the bed. "I brought you something for supper." The words rang out in a raspy voice that burned his swollen throat. "Help yourself, my dear. No need to say grace tonight." With his last ounce of strength, Patrick shoved Joss' body towards his marital bed.

The knees of Joss' body hit the edge of the bed, but rather than attempting to flee, it remained frozen in place, staring at the creature desperately fighting to be free of its restraints. Joss screamed and lashed out at his physical body to trigger some sort of response. It was then that the thing twisted onto its hands and feet to face Joss. Sticky trails of foamy saliva dribbles down her chin as she readied itself to pounce on Joss' rigid body. Its black craterous eyes stared through Joss to find the spectral being hovering far beyond. A smile cracked across its dead flesh, showing long razor-sharp teeth. It sprang onto Joss' body and sunk its serrated teeth deep into his flesh. They toppled backwards into the carnage and, with a sudden burst of blood, the demon ripped open Joss' throat. Madness consumed Joss while he experienced his body being torn apart and eaten before his spectral eyes, with all his senses intact.

Patrick could feel his smile grow ridged and firm as he gingerly caressed his wife's back. His fingers traced the decayed flesh and cancerous boils with a loving tenderness. Rotten flesh peeled away at his light touch, yet a sense of pride and joy

129

washed over him knowing that he could still provide for the love of his life.

"You enjoy now, Maria. I'll be back shortly." He patted her gently on her shoulder and shambled out of the room. "I have much to do before this night is over," he mumbled to himself.

A sense of clarity filled his mind as he lurched down the dark hallway. The fever seemed to have run its course and a cool sensation began to flow through his body. Red and blue lights cut through the darkness of the house creating a strobe light effect, capturing Patrick's macabre dance of madness. He blindly gripped the family portraits in the hall to keep on his feet. Through the ringing of his ears, he could vaguely hear the sound of sirens resonating through his home. There was chaotic shouting as a group of shadowed figures rushed through the front door.

"You there, put the weapon down!" one figure yelled at Patrick while the others aimed their guns at his chest. "Drop it. Get down on your knees!"

Patrick cocked his head sideways in confusion. He looked down at the gun he still clenched in his hand then flashed the officers his rigor mortis smile as he continued to walk towards the intruders in his house. He shambled forward, raised the gun towards the men and six blasts echoed through the murky darkness. Patrick collapsed to the hallway floor. Black ichor pooled beneath his twitching corpse. He no longer felt pain. No longer felt anything. Only an insatiable hunger remained.

"Man down! Man down!" one officer yelled out as another called out into his radio, "Shots fired. Man down. Request ambulance immediately!"

"Does he have a pulse?"

"Ya, it's faint but..."

"Ah, shit... the mother fucker bit me!"

Death For Art's Sake

Dorothy Davies

I'd been trying for an age to get an interview with Laurent Scopes, the brilliant artist whose stunning abstracts were setting the art world on fire. So distinctively different, such in-depth use of the darkest of reds, browns and blacks – never any other colours - it had all of us determined to find out how he did it, what the secret was of his success.

Finally he gave way to my persistence. I rang the doorbell with anticipation and excitement coursing through me.

Laurent opened the door, faded blue jeans, ragged tee-shirt splashed with some of the reds and browns he uses, big smile and what seemed like a genuine invitation to go in, not just the polite one most artists use when their sacred inner sanctum – their studio - is invaded by hacks. Quite why I expected a floppy hat, large silly bow and elaborate clothes I have no idea, he was after all a modern painter. Perceptions linger, however, in the most cynical of minds.

"Come in!" Full of bonhomie and welcome. "Come straight through to the studio, you're just in time. A new painting's in progress."

How, I thought, you've opened the door, you're guiding me down endless corridors, or so it seems, and here I am in –

132

A huge white space splattered in red and brown and black. An odd smell met me, one I could not quite place. Incense burners set around the room were masking it to some degree. Then I saw what Laurent was referring to.

A large canvas was lying on the floor under a tarpaulin suspended from the ceiling. There were holes slashed in the tarp, from which came splashes of the red/brown colour, Laurent's trademark. The whole thing was shivering, that was the only way to describe it and, as it shivered, more paint fell on the canvas. As I stood watching a masterpiece being created, the shivering stopped and the tarpaulin became still. A final drop fell in the centre of the painting.

Laurent reached down for the canvas and stood it up against the wall, admiring it. "Here we go. This is called Death For Art's Sake." He smiled and tugged my arm. "Come, it's your turn to create a masterpiece."

"I – I don't..."

"You will."

I was spun round and my hands secured behind me with plastic ties. I spluttered and tried to fight but that's impossible without hands. All I did was unbalance myself and end up on the floor which made it easy for him to secure my ankles as well.

From my position on the floor I could look up at the tarpaulin. Something was bothering me, a good deal more than the ties, which might have been some kind of surreal S&M game he was playing, for all I knew. But being thrown into the corner of the room was surely not part of a game.

My head slammed against the wall and almost knocked me out, but I had to try and get through to him.

"Laurent..." I wanted to protest, I wanted to argue; I wanted to know what the hell all this was about.

He turned to me with a smile that chilled me to my backbone.

"None of you understand, do you? True art demands sacrifice! My time, my genius, your sacrifice!"

As he spoke he tugged the corner of the tarpaulin. It tipped and a body fell out, a naked body, its wrists and ankles secured with plastic ties and a huge amount of duct tape over its mouth. The body of a young fit man. With slash marks all over it.

And then, in a moment of stunning clarity, I knew what the smell was.

Blood.

Laurent smiled again, that same chilling smile.

"You see how genius is created? I bind them, I slash them; I let them toss and turn in the tarpaulin, trying to escape. Their blood pours out, it cascades here and there, it splashes; it marks. No two canvasses are ever the same. They are young, they are fit; they fight the dying. As they fight the blood pours. As they die, the blood stops dripping and the painting is done. Oh, for your article, not that you will live to write it, of course, I never do more than one canvas a week. That means you have seven days in which to contemplate your major contribution to the art world. That gives me time to

134

dispose of this useless lump of flesh out in the marshes and clean the place up before you become the star turn."

Death for Art's Sake.

It would have made a good title for a good article.

But as he said, I wouldn't live to write it.

I wondered what he would call the masterpiece that is me.

Sleep Tight

Leslie Gulvas

The desert wind had a voice. Some nights it whistled, some it cried, others it whispered. This time it howled. Laura silently cleaned the kitchen and listened to the wind, knowing it was possible he would come back tonight. As much as she dreaded his sporadic visits, she hoped he wouldn't be drunk and would remember to bring food. Laura doubted if anyone but her husband remembered she was being kept in this isolated ranch house.

The wind's violent voice reminded her of her helplessness. Laura had tried to escape once. It was after she'd lost the first baby. He found her and brought her back to this internment. After her daughter was born she didn't dare make the trek to the highway, so she managed as best she could.

Daisy sat at the desk working on her spelling, her pink tongue firmly held in the left corner of her mouth. The soft glow of the lamp lit her pale blonde hair. He was the only one outside this house who even knew their daughter existed. When he was displeased, he pointedly reminded Laura of this fact.

Wind driven sand hissed against the windows. The house was as orderly as she could make it. A crumb lay on the counter, so Laura scrubbed its length again. Chipped plates were neatly stacked in the cabinet, the few spices in the rack all could be easily identified, turned so the labels were in alphabetical order. The wind's chaos didn't get into her house.

Laura had just finished in the kitchen when Daisy raised her head.

"I hear something, mamma." She closed her book and looked at her mother in expectation. "Is it him?" The child's breath came in short gasps.

"It's probably just something broke loose and rattling." Laura had her ears boxed so many times she didn't hear well anymore. "You run upstairs while I check."

She stepped out of the front door. Motion drew her gaze, something, speckled brown and as high as her waist nearly filled the six foot width of the porch. Laura squinted in the light from the doorway, unable to imagine what she was seeing. The surface of the object seemed velvety in the faint light from the front room windows. It was too big to be a bear. It didn't walk, it slowly heaved forward in a rocking motion, moving steadily away from her along the porch. It left a shiny wet trail in its wake. Her mind refused to believe what she saw.

"Mamma?" Daisy said from the top of the stairs. "Is it him?" Her voice quavered. She never called her father daddy.

The front section of the thing shifted and a great yellow eye on a gelatinous stalk rose and turned to observe Laura. She jumped back through the door, slammed it and scrabbled at the lock that hadn't been used in years. It screeched and resisted her arthritic pressure. Laura heard a crunching noise as the chairs at the far end of the porch shattered under the weight of the thing outside. This was crazy, it couldn't be real.

"Momma?"

She needed to protect Daisy. "It's nothing, sweetie," Laura said in as normal voice as possible. "Just the wind. Go on up and read in bed." Laura's breath came in gasps before the lock's tiny brass handle finally turned.

Daisy, eyes wide, didn't question her mother. She obediently disappeared from the top of the steps.

She wanted to run to her daughter, but needed to find a weapon. The thing was too big to get up the stairs even if it came in the house.

The noise from outside thumped and slithered under the moan of the wind. Laura ran to the back door and nearly fell when her shoes hit the cracked linoleum

The thing had made it to the back porch. An eye, completely filling the bottom four of the window's nine panes, stared at her. The gauzy half-curtain did little to hide its lidless gaze. Laura grabbed her largest kitchen knife and clutched it flat to her chest. She moved slowly to the door, sliding her feet along the floor. The creature's eye tilted down to watch her hand fight with the lock. The rusted steel did not budge. The eye calmly observed her actions.

Never letting her gaze fall from the unbelievable thing outside, Laura stepped back to grasp a chair from the kitchen table. She dragged it to her with slow deliberate motions. The monster was silent. The wind wailed a warbling moan. The sliding chair bumped across the broken place in the tile with a thump. In a flash, a second eye joined the first, filling more of the panes. Laura picked up the chair, the knife still tight in her hand. She braced the back of the chair under the doorknob. The eyes tilted to see what she'd done, then both turned to look at her directly, only inches away.

Laura met the creatures gaze, thinking this couldn't be real. There was no sense of malevolence from those giant round pupils. Both eyes on their velveteen flocked stalks appraised her. She had the impression that they found her wanting, her dress too worn, her shoes scuffed. Was she was going insane?

"Don't hurt us," she whispered. The eyes tilted in apparent recognition of her words. Despite its unhuman visage, the thing's gaze was intelligent and exuded calm. After a moment of mutual regard, the eyes telescoped down and the mottled brown body continued undulating along the back porch.

"Mamma," called her daughter from upstairs. "Is everything all right?" The wind nearly drowned out her mouse-like voice.

"Of course, honey. I'll be up in a minute."

"It's early. Do I have to go to bed?" Daisy's asked hesitantly from above. The girl was reluctant to ask for anything, even when he wasn't home.

"No, dear, just stay in your room," Laura said, confident Daisy would accept any direction her mother gave.

Laura walked the length of the small house, keeping pace with the bumping sliding sounds of the thing. She clutched the knife out of caution as much as concern. The creature made no attempt to enter the house. She heard it round the corner and moved back up on the front porch, circling the building. The remains of the chairs rattled like broken bones as they were pushed into the yard by the thing's passage through the dark. As it passed around the corner of the building, she unlocked the front door and stepped out to listen for the sound of his truck. The comforting knife was solid and ready in her hand. There was no sound of the muffler-less pickup her keeper drove. The smell of nutmeg, along with dust and sage, filled her nose.

Wind shrieked and battered the old house. She could hear the thing thumping and sliding on the back porch and Laura marveled that she wasn't more worried. Her mouth set in a grim line when she realized why. A slime-oozing creature circling the house was less frightening than her everyday life with the man who kept her here. She backed into the house and relocked the door.

Laura's eyes were drawn to where the goo from her shoes had besmirched the floor. She slipped the knife into the waistband of her skirt, just in case. A clean floor was something she could do so she got out cleaning supplies. The creature's huge eyes on their separate stalks watched through the kitchen window as she filled the bucket and added cleaning soda. It continued its rounds of the house. She mopped the goo from the front room's cracked floorboards.

When she took the scrub brush to the rug, a giant eye rose up to observe her through the small window in the front door. She ignored it and let scrubbing fill her mind. She took the uncomfortable knife from her waistband and sat it on the table next to the front door. Finally, she cleaned her shoes and placed them with heels in a perfect line next to Daisy's.

The wind blew in fits and gusts that didn't seem to affect the creature's rounds. Either it would leave or it would try to break in. There was nothing she could do. She was used to having no choice. Laura went upstairs to check on her daughter. She always tucked the girl in. Tonight should be no different.

"Will he be back tonight?" Daisy asked. The girl slept better when her father wasn't home.

Laura smoothed back the girl's child-soft hair. "I don't know when he will be back."

"Will he ever let us go see other people?" This had become Daisy's most common question.

"I don't know, darling. I'll ask him." Laura gave her standard answer, although she knew she never would ask. "Now you sleep tight. Promise me you won't come downstairs tonight. If you need anything, call and I'll bring it to you." At least she could shield Daisy from worry about the thing circling the house.

Daisy nodded solemnly.

Laura tucked the covers neatly around her daughter, straightened the books on her shelf and shifted the rug perfectly parallel to the bed. She stopped in the doorway and, before she turned off the light, she said, "You remember I love you, don't you?"

"Yes, mamma. Night, night."

"Night, night. Don't let the bedbugs bite."

"Oh mamma, you're silly."

"I guess I am." Laura pulled the door shut. No matter what happened, she would protect her daughter.

For hours Laura pottered around the house doing useless things to stay occupied. The sounds of the creature continued. It raised an eye to observe her as it passed the windows of whatever room she was in.

She finally sat in the living room, exhausted, and picked up the mending to keep her mind off what was outside. The thing, she didn't know what to call it, slowed its rounds to watch her through the front window. Her hands made tiny stitches that almost looked like they were done by a machine. The faint odor of nutmeg filled the room. Laura smiled, thinking the thing smelled like Christmas cookies. The rhythmic bumping sliding noise of this night visitor became a soothing counterpoint to the howling gusts of wind. After a few hours with no change in its behavior, she imagined it was guarding her, like a slime spewing watch dog. She wondered again if she had finally gone mad.

The distinctive grinding roar of her husband's truck rounding the butte drowned out the sound of the wind. Headlights flickered in the front window.

Her new friend was in the back of the house. The man wouldn't see it from where he parked. Laura dropped her mending and ran to the kitchen, took the chair from under the doorknob and swung the door open. The visitor's soft side filled the entry. Two plate sized eyes popped up and swiveled back toward her.

"You have to go. He has a gun in his truck. He'll hurt you." She couldn't stand the thought of this amazing creature under his control. She pushed against the soft fuzz covered bulk in the door way, a part of her mind wondering why it wasn't slimy. Sand slid off on to her clean kitchen floor. Out front she heard the door of the truck slam. "Go, hurry!" She made a shooing motion with her hands and pushed its spongy side again. The cookie smell became stronger.

The thing humped away, disappearing into the darkness. She closed the door and realized the front door was still locked. He would be so angry.

Her husband started to pound, rattling the door in its frame.

She dashed to the front room. His snarling, congested face and scraggly beard filled the small window on the door. Laura fumbled with the lock, bumping the table next to the door, making something rattle. She looked down at the knife.

"Let me in, you stupid bitch!" He slurred his words. Spittle spotted the window. He slammed his fist against the door.

The lock released and Laura threw open the door, ready to flinch away from her husband's blow. The scent of cookies and beer wafted in. Her eyes rose to the mottled brown body arched overhead nearly touching the beams of the porch. The thing rolled forward and dropped.

"What the fu—" Her husband's voice cut off abruptly.

Laura registered a pair of legs in dirty jeans. She realized that he had new boots just before they disappeared into the unseen maw. Her savior leveled itself out like a dropped bowl of Jello with a husband sized lump in its middle. As it slid away, one great yellow eye turned back toward her glinting in the light from the door.

The wind fell silent.

Laura closed the door and put the knife on the table. She would rinse off the porch tomorrow, before she and Daisy left.

Lamb in Wolf's Clothing

S J Townend

"It's an old, steamer trunk. I've managed to squeeze it in the boot but it weighs a tonne; couldn't get the bugger undone."

I was on the phone to my wife. She'd asked about the trunk my estranged, recently deceased father had bequeathed me. Haven't seen him since I was fifteen; he just upped and left Mum and I in the middle of the night. No reason. He wrote every month to tell me he missed me but I only found out where he'd been hiding all these years via the solicitor handling his affairs.

I turned the trip into a weekend getaway for my son, George, and I. Neither of us had been to Cornwall before. Ten years back, as soon as I'd gotten sober and we fell pregnant with George, I promised myself I'd be the father mine never was.

"George is fine. He's in the back, fast asleep."

After collecting the trunk, we visited a nearby beach. Sat between the dunes at Trebarwith Stand whilst George dug sandcastles, I broke down. The grief of it all, the thirty years of rejection, the story of how Dad had done some hideous stuff to his own body before blowing his brains out, it hit me hard. I hadn't had a drink for ten years, but the wine list in the beach café sung out like a siren that evening.

"Love, I've got to go. It's getting dark. The roads through these moors are windy and narrow—

I need to concentrate. I'll be home before midnight. Don't wait up."

The sun dropped below the horizon and a thick fog hung, but the guilt and the bottle of red I'd consumed were the real reasons I needed to end the call.

I dropped my phone into my lap. In my rear view mirror, I saw George, slack-jawed, asleep, blurry, in his child seat. My eyes flicked back to the dim road ahead. My body lolled from side-to-side with the sway of the country roads until a noise distracted me from my drowsy state.

It sounded like quiet rainfall at first; a repetitive pitter-patter which came up from behind and then dissipated on passing my window. Was something running alongside? I couldn't see much left or right and outside was growing darker by the minute. I squeezed the steering wheel a little tighter to keep myself awake. That's when I first saw it.

A yellow light suspended in the darkness ahead grew larger. Around it, I could make out the silhouette of something the size of a large deer bounding towards me. I was too hammered to hit the brakes in time. The thing outside, locked onto its target, was determined to take on my hatchback.

BANGTHUDSHUDDERTHWACK.

My body lurched forward. The air-bag mushroomed and caught my face. I slammed my brakes on and my tyres screeched out in the night. I pulled in, whacked on the hazards and turned to check on George—still fast asleep.

After my heart settled, I yanked out the spent air bag, double checked on my boy and got out of

146

the car. With only the light of the hazards flashing and my phone torch on, I stepped out into the dark country lane and walked back. What had I hit? Did I need to call its owner? God forbid, did I need to reverse and finish it off? I felt sick with panic. I prayed to find wildlife and not someone's beloved pet.

My stomach churned. Whatever it was, it wasn't moving. My drunken legs carried me over to the black heap thirty metres behind my car and crouched down at its side.

My brain tried to fight the sway the Merlot had brought to my vision. I focused on the injured creature I'd hit. It was still breathing, black-bodied and covered in fur or hair of some sort. Blood was leaking from it over the pocked tarmac like an inflating crimson balloon. My trembling torchlight slid along its contours and it hissed at me. In shock, I screamed and fell back.

It whipped round its neck to reveal a face.

Then she spoke.

"Bury me," her reedy voice whispered. On one side of her near-skeletal face, rended flesh like raw meat hung from her cheek bone. My heart started to beat double pace. I hadn't hit a cat, or a deer. I'd hit an old woman.

"Bury me," she croaked again and lifted a thin arm to wipe the blood and matted hair from her face. She opened her eye.

I staggered back and contemplated running to the car. I could've just disappeared into the night, pretended it never happened. But I couldn't—I'd taken an oath as part of my medical training. I'd never seen someone so elderly, so emaciated and so mangled survive such an injury. She was bleeding out, fast. I'd go down for manslaughter. Ten years minimum. I was definitely over the limit. Fear or guilt or house red rooted my feet to the spot. I had to help her.

"Christ. I'm so... sorry."

"Bury me," she said again.

Her thin legs were smashed to smithereens and folded in unnatural angles. Fractured bones jutted out through heavily haired skin. Sinew, yellow-white swathes of exposed fatty tissues, dripping tendons, rivulets of blood all kaleidoscoped before my sozzled eyes. I edged closer to try and assess her injuries. A ripple of intestines spooled out onto the road.

She was naked and covered in not dirty black bruises but patches of dark hair. She was in a state. At some point she'd lost an eye. Her single, yellowed eye stared into the very soul of me, then it rolled back in its socket. She started to cough and choke. A thick ribbon of blood erupted from her thin lips.

The trained medic in me took over. I placed my fingertips on her neck to try and take her vitals. The moment my fingers made contact with her flesh, her jaw sprang agape. She snapped at me, almost taking my fingers clean off. I pulled away fast and heard her rotten needle teeth crunch and crumble on impact. Her head tipped back. She let out a guttural sigh along with a foul stench before her body started to convulse. I felt helpless. After a hopeless minute which felt like an hour, I checked for a pulse and found none. Her skin felt not cold, but not warm either. Not warm enough, anyhow. Dead. I'd killed her.

Her final words were at sea in my head: *Bury me*. Who was this mad old hag? Who walked down a country lane in the cold of night, alone, naked, in the sticks?

I didn't want to go to jail—I could not miss George growing up. The events that followed her death seemed coordinated by a power higher. I, for certain, did not act rationally.

I grabbed the sandcastle spade and then wrapped her frail body in a beach towel. She weighed less than George so I hoisted her onto my shoulder. I stepped through the overgrown country ditch and into a fallow field, dumped the bag of dripping flesh and bones down and started to dig.

***

It was a shallow grave, all I could manage and who was going to look for her? No-one would have any clue I'd hit her, would they? And I was just doing what she'd asked me to do, wasn't I?

I dug and dug, fuelled by momentary madness and alcohol calories. Two or three hours passed. When the body lay two foot below, I changed into clean clothes, bundled my mud and blood stained clobber into a carrier, sunk a half-litre water, vomited and then drove the rest of the journey home, crying. What the fuck had I done?

We got home in the small hours of the morning. I bathed and wept, then slept fitfully.

149

Nightmares ensued: the lady's cycloptic face, her blood-mangled hair, her frail fur-covered body with its unravelling intestines, snapped bones jutting through ruptured viscera. The events of the night ran like horror footage back and forth through my mind. I tossed and turned until the sun rose.

In the morning, Gina took George to school and went to work before I pulled myself out of my sweaty pit. After a strong coffee, I burnt the bag of bloodied clothes in a fire pit in my garden. Whilst I watched the flames lick away the evidence, I remembered the trunk from my father.

I didn't have long until I needed to start my shift, but if it was full of junk, I wanted to burn it all, there and then, so I could forget about the whole weekend. I got some tools from the garage and attempted to pick the lock.

I gave in fast, my patience was thin. I grabbed an axe and swung the weighty blade at the lock of the trunk without even bothering to lift it from the boot, my back buggered from grave-digging. Blistered and sore hands ripped off the splintered wood panels from the lid of the trunk and tossed them on the fire. Then I saw a mass of dark fur inside the trunk.

My heart came up into my mouth. For a split second, I saw her again, the old woman. I contemplated swinging my axe down hard into the contents of the trunk, but I refrained. On closer examination, it was only a lifeless, silvery-grey pelt.

I lifted it out and unfurled the revolting coat. It was huge and stank of rot. Its lining was more

150

moth-hole than cotton and the brown stains on it crusted and clumped its silvery-grey striped pattern. I chucked the stinking jacket back into its lidless casket and a slip of yellowed paper fell from it to my feet. I read the note:

'*Wear me.*'

No chance. I screwed the note up and tossed it on the fire. I wanted to torch the coat too, but I knew the fur would've sent out billowing clouds of disgusting smoke and brought unwanted attention from neighbours. the old coat WAS back in the trunk and the trunk stuck in the boot of my car. I got ready for work. A fourteen hour shift in the trauma ward lay ahead of me. With less than three hours kip under my belt and a mind full of murderous guilt, the coat and trunk could wait.

***

"Mark, triage in cubicle six please." My boss said. "Then take a break. You look like shit."

I was shattered. All I could think about was the woman's face, her broken frame disappearing beneath clod upon clod of shovelled dirt and the strong desire to try and blot it all out with booze.

I was exhausted. I pulled back the blue curtain on cubicle six. The old lady. The dead woman I'd buried twelve hours lay there on the hospital gurney. Her jagged, broken limbs were folded like a pretzel. I could smell the moors, I could smell her rotting flesh; I could see maggots dancing in her wounds.

Acid rose in my throat. I could see her horrid face in more detail. Under the bright strip light she had whiskers. Two triangles of black velvet poked up from the top of her head underneath a mass of tangled jet black hair—ears.

She rolled onto her side; bones cracked and severed, clinging muscles strips snapped as she went. A long, black, feline tail swished out from behind her. She stared into my psyche with her single eye, as clear and burning yellow as a hell pit, and spoke.

"Thank you for burying me. My transformation is nearly complete."

Her ancient female shape shifted and throbbed and doubled in size. Black fur sprang from what had been split-open oozing skin. Her hands and feet became weighty paws with razor sharp claws.

It panted as I backed away from the bed. It curled up the top of its thick black lip to reveal a sardonic sneer of blade like dagger-teeth. A slug of drool dangled from the corner of its snout as it growled.

I turned and ran.

***

I jumped in the car, grabbed George from school. No plan. I needed him by my side before I put as much distance between us and the undead creature as I could. I left the city centre and hit the A road to Gina's work. I turned to look at George, he was confused and when I turned back round, that's when I saw it again.

152

"Shit," I screamed. "Hold on, George!" This time I sped up toward the black beast which pounded toward me.

The beast slammed into my front bumper, rolled up and over the windscreen and roof and thwacked down into the road behind us.

I must've been doing at least seventy on impact. I must've destroyed it.

"What is it? Why did you speed up like that, Dad?"

"Didn't you see it? Don't look back." He looked back.

"There's nothing there."

I saw the ruined pile of black fur and bloody bones in the road in my rear view mirror. "Don't you see it?"

"See what? It's just the road, Dad," said George. His body cranked round. "What's this gross grey thing in the boot? It stinks." He pulled the fur coat onto his lap and rummaged in its pockets.

"Leave it, son." I lessened my foot on the accelerator. Was it all behind me now—literally and figuratively? I bloody hoped so. I leant forward to peek through a clear spot in the windscreen which was cobwebbed with fractures.

"Is it wolf skin? There's a note in the pocket."

"What? Pass it to me."

I yanked the hand-written letter from its envelope.

Son,

153

As the eldest survivor in our blood line, it's with great sorrow I hand to you the burden and responsibility that I have born for what feels like an eternity. A longstanding hex looms over our family. You must wear the coat of wolf pelts to keep the Beast of the Moor at bay. It is our curse, our honour, and our duty. Remove the coat and it will hunt and kill, starting with you, followed by anyone who crosses its path.

I am so sorry.

Forever you have been loved and in my thoughts,

Your father.

My eyes flicked to the rear view mirror. Several hundred metres behind us the black beast, with the musculature and prowl of a black panther or jaguar or something in between and worse, started to lift its limbs, one by one, up and off the tarmac. I watched it shake its broken bones back together and, once more, pound down the road toward us.

I tossed the letter to the passenger seat. My addled mind tried to make sense of my fibbing eyes and my father's words. The coat—did I need to put on the coat?

"Give me the coat," I shouted and un-clicked my seat belt, then trapped the steering wheel by my knees and elbows. I slid my right arm through. God, it reeked of decay. My heart bashed in my throat. George was crying. He begged me to slow down. I pulled and tugged the pelt behind me as my car swerved. I rammed my left arm through.

154

The disgusting jacket clamped onto my chest like a vice. All the air left in me was forced out by its squeeze. I felt it adhere to the exposed skin of my arms and neck like limpet glue. It was as if the wolf pelts were melding to me, mingling with my own flesh and blood. The buttons seemed to fasten themselves. With the last one done up, I felt suddenly empowered. A rush of iridescent velvet shot up my spine and I howled at the day moon, a cloudy disc in the grey sky. From his child seat in the back, George cheered and laughed at my feral behaviour. I seemed to have no control over it.

I looked back. Before my eyes, the beast which had been gaining on us, turned to black dust, a soot-storm of static and dropped to the road, only to be blown away by the turbulence of the car's engine.

***

So this was it. Thirty years of letters, of Christmas and birthday gifts from my father, all with no return address. All those nights listening to Mother cry herself to sleep. It made sense. But it all didn't make any sense at all. I had a fur jacket which I needed to wear... forever... to keep this crone-bitch-cat-beast from shredding up me and my family? This was my calling? Had I lost the plot? I felt ill. Sick. Wanted a drink. Wanted to see Gina and have her tell me everything was going to be okay, that I was delirious, in a dark dream-state like I'd been when I'd gone through detox in the rehab centre years ago. But inside, I knew this wasn't imagined. This wasn't a hallucination.

***

I turned up at her work and looked at her with my red face. Drips of sweat rolled from my brow and chin. I explained what had happened after the beach, in the field of eternal midnights with the spade and the body, at work, on the road moments before.

"What are you wearing?" She turned her nose up in disgust.

"The coat Dad left me. Forever. Got to wear it. Keep it on. All the time." My words spilled out in stops and starts, a cluster-fuck of confusion.

She came up close. I wanted to take her in my arms, but she sniffed me and pushed me away. "You've been drinking."

"Not since last night," I said, but it was too late. She'd given me too many second chances. She told me I had until she finished her shift to clear all my stuff out from the house. She didn't want to see me ever again. I begged and pleaded to no avail. I tried to explain what had happened but my words sounded like the ramblings of a madman, a drunk. She gave me the silent treatment. I felt my sanity fray at the edges and my heart crack as I kissed my son goodbye.

***

It's been months since that day, the saddest day of my life. I've tried to take the coat off, but it comes, the she-beast. I hear it growl and gnash its teeth at me. I feel the thunder of its paws pounding the ground as it runs towards me. So I keep the coat on.

***

I keep myself to myself. I only exist to move to the corner-shop and back to my flat again. I know I stink, I'm filthy. I'm the local weirdo you cross the street from, the one who wears the hideous jacket, but I didn't deserve this unprovoked beating.

Here I am, lying on the pavement: ripped jeans, blood-stained t-shirt, stinking coat of wolf fur. I'm as drunk as they come. I can see my arm is snapped, my lip is fat. I've two black eyes. Did I hit my head? They really stuck the boot in this time.

I'm glad I've already drunk half a bottle; it's helping to numb the pain. I watched the rest of it smash and spray all over the street. That hurt the most.

Blue lights are bouncing off the buildings and I can hear the scream of sirens. The ambulance is pulling up beside me. All I can think about are George and Gina. It's been thirty-two years. My estranged son, my boy, George, will have turned forty. God, I miss them.

"Hello, Mr—? I'm Sam. This is Jane. We're paramedics. We understand you've been attacked by a gang of thugs. Can you tell us your name?

"Mark," I reply.

One of the paramedics shoots the other a confused look. It's as if they haven't understood me. Maybe they haven't. I am half-cut, half-broken.

"Sam. I can't understand what he's saying. He's inebriated. Alcohol?"

"I'd say."

"Looks like we've a broken arm, facial injury, bump to the head. Let's bring out the stretcher, neck brace. I'll strip him down, get some fluids in."

The taller of the pair, his nose scrunched up in disgust at the smell emanating from my unwashed body, is coming at me with scissors. He starts to snip off my coat. I'm flailing my uninjured arm about to push him away whilst letting out a wail of disagreement. No. He can't take it off.

"Don't take off my coat," I mumble.

Snip. Snip. Tear. Rip.

Damn, it's too late. He's cut right down each arm and ripped open the buttons. He's pulling it off me. I try to resist but the other one is restraining me. They're putting something sharp into my arm.

That's when I see it, for the final time, with its single, jaundiced devil's eye, its pounding paws, its snarl of razor sharp teeth. It's charging towards me, on target, hungry, free.

The Yew's Dark Secret

Michael B Fletcher

'Centuries.' Our guide stopped and dramatically raised his arm. 'I'm told, centuries old.' He pointed into the sky.

'What's he talking about?' I asked my girlfriend holding onto my arm.

'Don't know but my feet are killing me. Can't we sit for a while? Make a change from listening to his rabbiting on. Everything in this god-damned place is centuries old anyway. What's one more thing?'

'See the way it's broken apart the rock. Makes you wonder at its power and longevity, eh?' His voice washed over us as I sought to find something to sit on. If Julie had sore feet, then she'd let me know all about it and I'd suffer tonight, I know I would. The money I'd spent on the tour and tonight's hotel didn't bear thinking about, although I thought I could cancel the restaurant, get take-away or something. Save a bit and still get my way in the end.

I spied a flat piece of stone, large enough for us both yet near enough so we could still hear our guide's pearls of wisdom.

I tugged on Julie's arm, wondering how such a pretty girl could look so plain when she was pissed. 'There's a spot to sit. We can still listen from there.'

'What?' She had turned away. Apparently our boring guide was saying something of interest. Maybe my outlay wasn't going to be wasted after all.

I looked back to the slab of stone, wondering if I could lead her to it while her attention was elsewhere - my feet were beginning to hurt too now.

'Did you hear what he said?' she whispered in my ear as I manoeuvred her to the stone.

'What?' I was attempting to show some interest as we sat.

'The tree, the one we're sitting under, it's centuries old.'

'So? You said you didn't like the centuries bit.'

'I know what I said!' she snapped. 'You are a fool, Jason.'

Bugger, I thought, *it's back to take-away*.

'It's just what the tree is. Why it's growing here.'

'A tree's a tree. What does it matter where it is?' I looked around at the piles of stonework in various stages of decay dotting the ancient graveyard.

'Oh!' she hissed. 'Just listen.'

I briefly wondered whether I could get my deposit back from the hotel as I turned my attention to the guide.

'Investigations have revealed that one of the city's most vile people in the twelfth century, accused of murder, rape and incest, was buried there. Further studies have indicated he was the reason for the yew tree being planted where it was.'

160

'Did you hear that, Jason? He was why the tree's here. An incestuous monster. How thrilling!'

I resolved to pay more attention. Maybe my plans for tonight weren't wasted after all. 'So, what sort of tree is it?' I'd missed that bit.

'It's a yew.' She turned, her face flushed with excitement. 'And they say it was planted here to keep the evil man in his grave.'

'Ha.'

Her eyes hardened.

'I mean, huh. Can't be the real reason, though, can it?'

'Yew trees are really mysterious. If you cut them they have blood in them, in the uh - heartwood. That's what he says. And he also says it has special qualities. If you... if you chew some of its leaves at night, in the graveyard you can feel the very essence of the man coming through.'

'Whose? The murderer bit? I probably wouldn't mind the incest, but murder?'

'Ha ha!' She laughed before tilting her head and looking up into the gnarled branches.

Amazing how she could change. At one stage she was getting cranky with me, the next, with the thought of a good mystery, she became a great companion.

'Why don't we, then?' I put some intrigue into my voice.

'Why don't we what?' Her green eyes laughed into mine.

'Do it. Come back tonight and do it.'

'Do you mean, chew the leaves?. See what they taste like?'

161

'What else?' *What else*, I thought, having a fair idea.

So we had a good meal at a chic restaurant with Julie going on about the coming adventure, virtually non-stop. Several glasses of wine probably added to the sense of excitement. The night was balmy with no sign of a moon. We made our way back to the graveyard. I admit I was glad no-one could see us as what we were doing was a bit of a prank. Once we'd chewed a leaf or two I'd be heading straight back to the hotel for the rest of the night's entertainment.

It looked different at night. The tumbles of broken graves and mausoleums lit by my torch added to the eerie atmosphere, the only things moving were the two of us. Everything had gone quiet, our footsteps the only sound.

'Different, eh? In the dark?' I held Julie close as we moved into the graveyard. 'Why don't we just grab a leaf off the tree and then eat it back at the hotel?'

'What? My brave adventurer scared of the dark?'

Julie really pissed me off when she said that, but it was night-time and she couldn't see my face. So I followed her confident stride through the lines of decaying tombstones towards the skeletal branches of the ancient yew.

'Could've eaten them in the daylight,' I said.

'No fun then,' said Julie. 'Besides he said it had to be at night for it to work.'

'You're not joking, are you? You really believe we'll be able to taste something?'

'We'll see.'

'Bugger,' I mumbled.

Close up the tree had a real presence and, if I wasn't me, I'd have been nervous because it was kind of spooky.

'Here.' She thrust a piece of branch in my face. 'Only chew a few needles as it's poisonous and we don't want to overdo it.'

'What? You never said it'd be poisonous.'

'You didn't ask. Anyway it's only a little bit. I'm trying some.'

I watched her as I tentatively placed several spikey needles in my mouth. The bitter taste overwhelmed my senses and any hope I might have had of detecting a spectral presence was gone in an instant.

I could hear Julie chewing as I spat into the dark.

'Eugh, it even tastes poisonous.'

Just then the tree moved in a sibilant rustle of needles. I backed away. shining the torch up into the branches. 'What was that?' I tried to see into the foliage but the dark seemed to press down, weakening the light.

'Must be a bat or something? Shit!' My foot hit a rock and the torch fell to the ground with a clatter. The light went out.

'Julie? Julie, did you bring a torch? Mine's busted.' I reached around behind me and grasped the edge of a drunken-leaning gravestone, listening intently.

'Julie?' My voice rose. 'You stupid bitch! Stop playing silly buggers.'

She didn't answer.

The darkness was intense. I blinked frantically to get some night vision. shuffling around the gravestone, keeping a grip on it.

I gulped, trying to still my breath. 'Where are you?' My voice broke the silence.

I listened, hearing only the faint drip of moisture off the headstones and the creak of the tree over my frantic heartbeat.

A faint light in the graveyard, maybe from a fungus or some such helped me see, even though I wished I hadn't. The decaying structure of monuments and stonework celebrating the dead was shadowy and menacing, each space between black and bottomless. And above it all, as if presiding over some ancient burial rite, the dark mass of the yew tree.

No sign of Julie.

I spat again, trying to rid my mouth of the acrid taste before edging away from the gravestone, one foot at a time. No point in calling out for my traitorous girlfriend, I just wanted out of this hideous place.

I headed back where I thought we'd come, bumping into headstones, treading on god knows what all the while seeking the way out. At one stage I even scrambled over a mound of earth rising from a grave.

By now my head was throbbing, breathless, my stomach muscles clenched to stop my guts from rebelling. 'Must be nearly there,' I murmured and squeezed between two eroded columns.

'Ah, a path.' I stepped onto a lighter line in the dark. I took two more paces before looking up, expecting to see the ironwork marking the boundary of the graveyard.

'Oh shit!' A spiky branch touched my face. I fell against the massive trunk of the yew tree, stomach roiling and heart threatening to burst.

My mind almost closed down when I felt the rough bark at my back. I pulled my knees into my chest, shivering and panting, eyes clenched shut.

I must've stayed like that for a while until I noticed a glow. A quick peek made me regret opening my eyes, for there was a light rising from the graves. A scream built in my throat even as my traitorous stomach released its burden.

The light was dazzling. I heard a familiar voice call. 'Jason? Where are you? I've got the spare torch.'

'Julie?'

I tried to reach out to snatch the torch off her but she went straight past.

'Here, you stupid bitch!' I screamed to her back, outlined by the glow. 'Back here!'

She kept going, the light bobbing and flickering amongst the headstones. 'No!' I attempted to scramble to my feet but I couldn't move. 'Bloody sticky sap.'

I tried again to yell but the taste of the yew filled my mouth and stopped my voice. I heard the rasp of the needles as I tried to move my hands. All I could see between my legs were rough coarse roots stretching out. Fear coursed through me as I heaved with all my strength to get away from what was happening. My mind flickered between consciousness and a desire to close down. *No,* I thought, *it can't be. I'm a man.* The tree shuddered through me and I slipped into a darkness filled with sinister whispers.

Slices

Neil Baker

It was freezing, despite the fact the sun had risen, blasting splintered shafts of amber through the tops of the aspens bordering the playground. For Jenny, it had already been an intolerably long morning and it was barely 8:00 am. She tightened her grip on the old wooden planks either side of her head and tried, fruitlessly, to gain a better purchase with her right foot barely hooked onto the metal bar at the top of the helter-skelter. Her left foot probed gently for another secure anchor, but found nothing, just like the previous half-dozen times she had tried. Each attempt caused her to slip a little more, dropping her inch by squeaking inch down the spiraling slide and closer to the scores of razor and scalpel blades that studded the slippery surface like dozens of dorsal fins in a glassy sea. She tried once more to push back with her arms, but her strength had long abandoned her. Her shoulders burned and her forearms shook. Her knuckles, taut and pale, stood out like tiny rivets on the curved, grey oak and as she strained, her left hand slid forward - a combination of exertion and a bloody, sweaty slickness. Jenny gasped as she descended slightly and craned her head away from the closest blades that sat glued at a jaunty angle, mere inches from her face. Her right foot still maintained its tenuous latch, but she knew it wouldn't be long before it broke free, since it was bearing most of her weight.

The soundtrack to Jenny's predicament was frustratingly chipper. Black-capped chickadees provided an acapella melody to the relentless percussion of downy woodpeckers hidden against the bark.

A small number of the tiny chorus had left their leafy confines and were now hopping merrily across the playground, flipping cork chips with their beaks in the pursuit of breakfast. Jenny watched them, hating them for their uselessness. A short squeal, like the air being released through the neck of a stretched balloon, signaled that she was on the move again and Jenny's body shuddered forward. She cried out as an oaken splinter pierced the palm of her right hand and then she gripped harder. Stupidly she had allowed herself to be distracted by the birds. She strained to look over the edge of the slide, but the wooden walls blocked her peripheral vision. All she could see ahead of her was a rusted swing set, a neglected bench, the row of aspens and then the solar-paneled roofs of her street, lurking furtively beyond the foliage. Stainless steel shards dominated the foreground and it was becoming harder to ignore their gilded edges. For the first time in her life, Jenny felt regret.

Jenny was eight when she first cut her mother.

This small act of utter maliciousness had been born of curiosity. She had loved Mother, still did, but the opportunity had gnawed at her ill-sprouted soul until she felt compelled to act on it. The idea had formed while she watched Mother wash the dishes. Mother always left the glasses until last, refilling the sink with fresh water, then cleaning each one with a curved flourish as she wiped the sponge around the interior, three fingers on the sponge and her thumb and pinkie finger chasing each other around the edge.

One evening, Jenny had taken one of the glass tumblers into the basement and, using Father's tool that looked like a skinny alligator, managed to make a barely perceptible nick on the rim. When she replaced it among the pile of dirty plates and mugs, Jenny made sure to hide the crack with a smear of bacon fat from the rim of the skillet. Then she watched and waited.

Mother filled the sink, washed and rinsed the plates and mugs, dropped in the cutlery and then reached for the glasses. To Jenny's delight, mother selected the booby-trapped tumbler first. She held it under the suds for a second; then drew it up and began to clean with the sponge. Jenny spotted the blood first - perhaps the hot water had masked the initial pain - but mother soon reacted with a flurry of contortions as she dropped the glass into the sink in a pink, foamy explosion. She cried out, more in astonishment than pain and held her hand high. For a fleeting moment, Jenny could see the injury as a scarlet silhouette against the window. The skin between mother's pinkie and ring finger had been cut deep; as mother splayed her digits, the gap between them seemed unnatural - and exhilarating.

A stabbing twinge in Jenny's lower back made her spasm and she gasped as she slid forward another inch. Instinctively, she slapped her right hand onto the face of the slide and realized her mistake immediately. Her glossy palm slipped on the metal surface and the foremost blade sliced away the knuckle skin from her forefinger. Jenny screamed and lifted her bloody hand before it could slide into the next row of waiting blades, forcing it against the side of the curved wall as her body twisted to compensate for the uneven support. This halted her descent, but if the renewed shaking in her arms was any indication, this was a temporary halt. A tear-smeared glance revealed no one rushing to her aid. She doubted anyone had heard her cry and she was thankful for that.

There was little connective tissue between the subsequent recipients of Jenny's 'research', other than proximity and opportunity, but sometimes the results of her traps were made all the sweeter due to happy accidents. There was the time when she was ten years old.

She had laced father's basement pool table with a tiny, spring-mounted scalpel blade that would lay flush against the leather-lined corner pocket when a hand was inserted but would pop out upon withdrawal. She had assumed it would be Father's sinew and meat revealed under the bright glare of the pendant lamp, but it had been the pudgy fat of Uncle Darren's back hand. This sat well with Jenny, since Uncle Darren had often rested that same clammy hand on her thigh at dinner time. The large man howled, balling his wounded fist and widening the tear - further exposing the blood and fat-globule seepage like rhubarb in custard - and Father despaired at his stained baize. Jenny surreptitiously

170

reached into the scarlet-stained hole and unhooked the blade and its retaining pin, secreting them into her pocket as she exited hastily under the pretense of looking for a box of band aids. She was always careful to remove the evidence.

Jenny's fascination with the abject was tempered only by her desire not to be caught and so she abstained for a few months between each maiming, carefully considering her next victim and the method she would employ. Both Mother and Father were wounded during the remainder of the year, usually on the foot or ankle, each time attributing the lacerations to jutting screws or faulty furniture and neither suspecting their daughter. It was only a matter of time before Jenny took her work to other places; she had a wealth of subjects to choose from. She could target the Bellemys; a trio of obnoxious boys who lived in the house next door.

It was impossible to ignore them. The constant squawking from their backyard as each brother grew louder to attempt dominance during their games over their siblings was intolerable.

Whenever Jenny escaped to the park for a moment of solitude with her sketchbook, the Bellemys seemed to follow, launching themselves upon the helter skelter and pushing each other down the corkscrew slope with ear-splitting cries of *'Geronimo!'*.

Jenny had frequently imagined them all tumbling down the slide, emerging at the bottom in a mess of screams and shredded legs. Before this would take place, though, she had settled on a more immediate nuisance.

Denyse *'Denny's'* Sterling was the variety of school bully who firmly believed in hitting all the right notes along with all the right kids. She was thick of stature and mind, commendably committed to an awkward fashion style all her own and had taken ownership of her nickname with aplomb. In fact, she reveled in the moniker; the beatings she dished out on a daily basis were known as the 'over easy', the 'scrambler', the 'early morning special' and the 'lumberjack' although the latter form of assault was rare, due to its reliance on an implement. Jenny had no real beef with Denyse – she had never been targeted herself- but the girl preyed on the weak and was a malignant creature of habit, so she became the next subject.

Every school day ended the same way as the students filed out the main doors. *'Denny's'* would appear at the top of the steps and launch herself onto the central wooden handrail, flopping over like a bag of wet sand before sliding down to the pavement on her stomach. There she would dismount and whale on whoever was unfortunate enough and small enough to be at the bottom and therefore that afternoon's victim.

Jenny had chosen the first Friday in September to pull off the experiment. Her thinking was if it worked, Denyse would be out of commission almost immediately, a nice start to the school year.

She had excused herself twenty minutes before the end of day with 'stomach cramps' (never questioned) and sloped out of the school to set up her device. It was a beautiful little contraption that she had spent a week creating,; a scalpel blade attached to a spring-loaded arm that fit snugly into a shallow groove which she had surreptitiously carved out of the handrail over the past four days. Then she stood just inside the doors, longing for the bell.

The students piled out of their classrooms and thundered out of the building, a mass of swinging backpacks and inane chatter. Jenny saw Denyse stamping down the corridor and timed a turn so that she walked a few paces before the bully. Jenny skipped down the steps, pausing momentarily to raise the trap and then stepped to one side. On cue, *Denny's* flung herself over the wooden rail and began her whooping descent. There was a faint ripping sound as she passed over the blade (*was it clothing or skin?*), and Jenny deftly sidestepped back to the center of the steps to retrieve her device. It was wet and a little tricky to pull out, but it eventually did so, just as Denyse reached the bottom with a gurgled cry. Jenny turned in time to see the girl stagger to her feet, crimson hands held tightly to her belly and then watched as a tiny loop of something purple dangled from the front of Denyse's jacket before she collapsed. A great success.

It felt like hours had passed. In reality, probably only a few minutes, but hanging on for grim life tends to distort your perception. Jenny grimaced and exhaled through clenched teeth. She could feel

173

the strength leeching from her arms and the trembling had become horrendous. As her muscles weakened so did her resolve and a pang of regret began to stir, the first time she had ever experienced such a feeling.

If only she hadn't allowed the Bellemys to rankle her so, if only she hadn't set her alarm for 6:00 am, if only she hadn't meticulously superglued over eighty blades of varying size and lethality to this spiraling slide. *If only*...

Then, a sound, the unmistakable squeals of small boys. The Bellemys. Jenny strained to see them, but her view was still blocked. The noises grew closer and she felt new strength in her shoulders and wrists, new air in her lungs. She shouted.

"Hey!"

The boys' yelling stopped, and she could hear them shuffling around in the bark chips at the base of the slide.

"Hey!" she repeated, "get up here and help me!"

"Jen?" It was the oldest brother, Caleb.

"Yeah, it's Jen. Can you come up and grab me? I'm stuck."

The boys giggled, then Caleb shouted back. "What you doing up there?"

Jenny could feel her anger rising, but she held it back. "Just playing. But it's busted."

"Playing?" The Bellamy brother sounded incredulous.

Jenny felt herself sliding again, just a few hairs but enough to elicit a furious yell.

"Just get up here!"

The laughter continued, but to her relief Jenny heard the brothers scuffling through the bark and then their footfalls upon the metal rungs of the helter-skelter ladder. A few seconds later she felt a hand on her ankle. The grip was not as strong as she expected, though. She tried to sound as grateful as possible.

"Great, now pull! Please."

"What ya doing?"

The voice was high-pitched and she realized it was the youngest Bellamy who held her life in his squidgy little palms.

"Get your big brother!"

"Why?"

Jenny inhaled deeply, ready to blast her demand again, when her left arm suddenly unlocked and she twisted onto her side, hitting her temple against the wooden wall. She slid forward, enough to nick her chin on the first blade and felt tears begin to well. She pleaded with the child.

"Just…"

A second hand grabbed her ankle and slowly began to prise it away from the metal rail it was hooked onto. *That's it*, vast relief washed over her, *pull me u…*

Her foot was lifted and then heaved with all the effort a seven-year-old could muster, as the youngest Bellamy sent Jenny on her way.

"Geronimo!"

Food For The Gods

Alaric Cabiling

The room was dark. Locrian unbuttoned his shirt.
Beads of sweat left wet tracks on his six-pack. He
lay back against the bed. The smoky air was alive
with excitement. He swept his fingers through his
hair, watching the door, waiting for something or
someone.

Cars on the street ground to a halt. There was a
collision, yelling. There was the sound of a cat
wailing, a child calling out to his mother in distress.
Locrian was in a Gentlemen's Club in historic
Jackson Ward in Richmond, Virginia—the Moulin
Rouge of the South in its heyday.

His car was parked outside, as was a woman's
old Jaguar.

The room was a role-player's special. The
bedsheets were red. The pillows were shaped like
hearts. The room smelled of cheap cologne and
sweat. A glass of bourbon sat on a tray beside a
bucket of ice cubes which were slowly melting, just
as Locrian's heart was pounding, blood surging
throughout his body. Anticipation built up steadily.
Locrian felt warm sweat trickle down his temples.

The door opened and total darkness greeted
him. Nothing could have been darker than that tear
in the fabric of space and time. Something in it
shifted, black in black, a shadow against darkness,
darkness moving in the absence of light. Locrian

heard muffled footsteps, then the crack of a whip! Lights came on and there she was—the woman he saw in secret, wearing black leather and black fishnet stockings.

She tied her blonde hair behind her head. She wore a black mask around her eyes, leaving the rest of her face bare: the sleek contour of her cheeks, her moist tongue licking her lips. They made up a perfect symmetry of parts.

She crept up towards him in bed, then straddled his leg. She moved so easily, flowing on top of him like water. He allowed her to do what she wanted. She slid a hand into his open pants zipper, summoning his pleasure, then took him in inside of her.

Locrian liked his fun and the woman felt certain of the same. Who was she? They met to spice up their sex lives; bored aristocrats who perhaps didn't know how better to pass the time. They didn't stay long after the rendezvous, leaving like strangers, only to part with smiles that suggested they would be meeting again.

***

A couple in a restaurant was dining on lamb shanks braised and roasted to perfection. They basted the lamb with a butter and garlic sauce that made the olfactory senses squirm with pleasure.

The bottle of wine was equally special. Damian and his wife, Dita, both had a glassful, toasting to the occasion - an acquisition of a profitable company in Rhode Island. It was another addition to their already sizable fortune.

They had chosen a restaurant recommended by friends in the Baltimore area. Damian chose Baltimore in particular for a reason unknown to Dita—to dine far from acquaintances in Richmond, Virginia and not be seen or heard from. They were dressed splendidly and so were the other patrons. The tablecloths were pristine and the glasses of wine were clear as crystal. A quartet played chamber music. The lush sounds of strings lulled hearts. The gentle tapping of keys wove a tapestry of colors beneath closed eyelids, some guests shutting their eyes to hear the music better.

The waiter was chosen especially for Damian and Dita by the maître d'. The waiter was often the recipient of the restaurant's biggest tips, due to his courtesy and outstanding service. He conducted himself like a gentleman, befitting the restaurant's clientele and effortlessly carried the serving tray with grace, like a ballet dancer holding out a hand to his partner.

He asked Damian and Dita if they were satisfied with the meal.

"Indeed, we are," Damian said. Dita looked up, smiled, and speared some more of the lamb on her plate.

"Yes, indeed," she replied to the waiter.

The waiter left, satisfied with his service. He looked forward to his tip.

In fact, the valet driver also expected rather sizable tips from Damian and Dita. They arrived separately, appearing like an unhappily married couple. Damian drove his Maserati Quattroporte—a full-size luxury sedan. Dita drove her Jaguar—a vintage 2-door XE that Damian's mechanic took special care to maintain.

"This night is special," Damian told Dita, who smiled back at him. There was sadness in his eyes as he looked at her, aware that there was something wrong. Suspicions slithered in and out of their lives, finding a crack or hole from which to escape.

She acknowledged his answer.

"I'm so proud to be your wife," she said.

They were spending the night at the Hyatt at the Inner Harbor. Damian looked forward to romancing his wife. At the hotel, Dita had more than her usual share of drinks before making love to Damian.

***

The next day, Damian was enjoying the lull in his schedule by playing golf with a friend. However, after the friendly match, Damian planned on driving back to his office, where his assistant was busy compiling reports for him to examine. Besides that, his company staffers needed his signature on a budget proposal, but he planned on putting the latter task off till Monday.

In the meantime, there was nothing pressing. The golf course was sunny and bright. The greens were lush and the sand traps were well-sculpted. Being the establishment's best patron and a friend of real estate mogul Locrian Sumner, another important patron, Damian always had the first crack at the golf course after maintenance did its job on Sundays, benefitting from the best conditions for playing.

Locrian had decided to brave the trip back from South Carolina that Monday in his Ferrari, enjoying the open Virginia air and the green lawns stretching for miles and miles outside Richmond City.

Locrian led through the first holes but lost the lead on the ninth when his nine-iron clubbed the ball towards the woods. Damian chuckled happily at the sight of his friend fuming as his shot went awry.

"Better luck next time," Damian said, walking with his friend to the edge of the wooded area, where he would wait for him to find the ball among twisted, gnarly roots and fallen conifers.

Locrian patted his friend on the shoulder and mused at what he called overconfidence. "I let you win," he said.

"Don't you always?"

Locrian looked everywhere for the ball but couldn't find it. His caddy shook his head when he looked over. Frustrated, Loki told Damian that Damian was indeed the winner, like the latter was in so many other matches, besides being the winner in a friendly competition for Dita's hand in marriage.

Locrian was so close to upending Damian; he was closer than he'd ever been in previous golf matches. Dita's decision to stay with Damian hinged on addition versus subtraction: Damian was richer; Locrian was jittery with the trigger when it came to tough business decisions. The two friends would take it out on friendly golf matches, but the two weren't close to living out a rivalry. Locrian had to win some to call it that.

"Dating anyone, Loki?" Damian had asked. Locrian shook his head.

"Girls are always easy. Finding the right one's hard."

"You will," Damian answered, consoling his friend.

"Just hope it doesn't end up doing you worse."

***

Dita drove up to the valet parking of the Jefferson Hotel in her 2 door Jaguar, wearing a sleeveless black dress. Her hair was tied up above her head, with some tresses winding down the side of her face. She looked stunning. She was the heiress, the stable decision-maker behind the ownership of several hotels, restaurants and cafes. She also flaunted her beauty like she was made to express perfection.

Waiting in the hotel bistro: Locrian Sumner. Not Damian.

They've been rendezvousing for some time. Sometimes meeting in seedy joints, in men's clubs, and in public bathrooms, the two adulterous lovers saw no limits to their search for cheap thrills.

This time, Locrian waited for her at the bistro in plain sight, knowing that Damian might have spies in the hotel concierge and staff.

They still got a room and made love like paramours starved for flesh. Dita couldn't believe her misfortune: married to the man her family convinced her would guide her sizable fortune to greater heights while enlarging his own, despite loving Locrian more.

At least, it was the thrill of the hunt she loved the most.

***

Damian and Dita had no children. She was unable to give him any. He gave her luxurious accommodations, fine automobiles, rooms in five-star hotels in all the most exotic places and Dita thought these extravagances were what she wanted.

But feeling empty, despite their wealth and affluence, she searched for something more in life. She was herself a businesswoman and their marriage was also a matter of addition versus subtraction. He had more assets than she did.

She wore the glamorous dresses he liked but yearned for those she preferred. She made love to him the way he wanted, but she longed for something more in the needling heat of passion besides merely surrendering her body to him, if only less than willingly.

Dita was beautiful, richer than her wildest dreams and had a husband who loved her, but she envied others who seemed ostensibly happier.

She found momentary excitement in the arms of her husband's close friend—Locrian Sumner, who was himself wealthy, had time on his hands and looked like a celebrity.

They made love on weekends while Damian was away on trips. Locrian told Damian that he, too, traveled often but, in fact, seldom did. Instead, he spent time with Dita, the woman he loved before he'd lost her to his friend. He had hoped that Dita would listen to her heart before arriving at a decision. Instead, Damian's stability and steady hand at plotting business decisions were too much for Dita to turn down. Locrian and Dita had their cheap thrills, meeting in sleazy bars and motels, pretending to rendezvous for fun. Dita would dress provocatively and all Locrian had to do was show up, wearing a smile that spelled out something illicit. With Damian, she had a man who steered the ship like the sails commanded the winds. With Loki, Dita played around like she was reliving her teen years.

What Dita and Locrian didn't know was that Damian had known all along the two of them were meeting in secret…

***

It was Friday again and Damian was going out of town on business. The couple prepared for his departure by packing, cooking, dining indoors and doing the salsa in the ballroom.

The large house was quiet. The water in the pool outside the house was still. The two showered together in the master bath, making love beneath the water falling from the spout. Then, they lounged in the tub and waded in the salt bath.

It was morning and Damian was due for his flight. He pretended to look at himself in the mirror as he combed his hair but instead watched his beautiful wife reach into her purse for her phone.

Later, Dita cooked him breakfast. She could flip the scrambled eggs like a chef. Despite the servants being given time off, the house remained remarkably tidy and the couple hadn't demonstrated any dependency on the hired help.

The two kissed outside before he drove off to the airport. Damian wore a white casual shirt with folded-up sleeves and creaseless beige cotton-twill pants. He waved goodbye but knew that the night's proceedings weren't likely to happen again. He knew a door was opening, the front door maybe, but felt that he was on his way out and someone else was coming in—that his wife didn't want him anymore.

He felt like fighting for what they had but wondered what that was. Maybe a lie... and a bank account that would have lasted generations—money someone else might have wanted from her.

Damian was smarter than that. He and Dita signed a prenup. Marital infidelity was cause for a much smaller settlement for the party with smaller equity in assets—Dita.

With Damian's car far down the road leading out of the estate and nowhere in sight, Dita immediately grabbed her phone and walked out onto the patio, which had a view of the pool.

She needed only to utter a quick word.

"It's me," she said.

***

Damian opened the door to his hotel room in Buenos Aires, looking forward to some respite. He went in and inspected the accommodations, seeing if the hotel staff met his requirements. He checked the bathroom and found the spa suitable. He checked the linen closet and found luxurious towels, softer than his own. He searched the bed and found his favorite mints on the pillow. "Perfect," he said less than enthusiastically.

Based on what he was wearing, Damian might have looked as if this wasn't a business trip. He thought that Dita hadn't noticed, or that perhaps she hadn't cared enough to realize that he was dressed for a leisurely excursion instead.

He unpacked and waited. He decided against room service, opting to go down to the bar and lounge where other patrons were.

The hotel's marble floors seemed blasé. The wallpaper seemed old.

He changed, getting into his Givenchy sport coat and matching pants. He wore a white Italian sport shirt inside. It occurred to him that he might have been subconsciously trying to tell Dita that he planned to cheat on her by dressing so casually for a business trip. He wanted to rouse her anger; anger would have been a sign that she still cared for him. He still wanted to save his marriage.

Instead, Dita seemed more concerned about meeting her lover than caring at all about what her husband was doing.

The lounge wasn't ready for Damian. He sat on a stool and ordered a scotch on the rocks. Heads turned. Eyes glistened.

"Something for the broken-hearted?" the bartender asked. Damian shook his head.

The bartender was well-dressed, fit, and well-shaven, but these traits might have been prerequisite for his job.

"What makes you say that I'm broken-hearted?" Damian asked the bartender, pretending to grin like it was preposterous.

"Scotch this early? This bar is only for hipsters," the bartender said with a chuckle. "Nobody wants to drown their troubles here. There are plenty of women, plenty of men like you, who in turn, have plenty of other women."

"Not me," Damian said flatly.

"Not yet," the bartender replied.

The bartender left Damian when another patron called for more drinks. In the bartender's place stood silence, a brash interloper in space.

A woman sat beside Damian. Damian said hello and the woman answered. They talked for a few minutes about the weather, then became curious about each other.

"Are you here on business?" she asked Damian.

"In Buenos Aires?"

She raised an eyebrow, still smiling. Anything's possible, she could have said, but she was waiting for Damian to surprise her. Damian sensed that the young woman could tell that he was wealthy. He could tell that she was deciding

186

whether he'd be interested in her. Her smile betrayed her intentions. Damian could tell that she wondered whether he would have fancied her for just a night, which might not have been worth the trouble.

He smiled. She had a naïve look to her, which Damian mistook for innocence. It was his scotch.

"My place isn't far," she told him. Damian considered the proposal only briefly. She seemed like a nice girl, just lonely, looking for love in all the wrong places—a bar that catered to passing acquaintances, meetings between colleagues, one-night stands.

Then, he thought of Dita.

"No," he said. "I can't. I'm sorry."

Damian had no idea what came over him. He was no swinging guy. He traveled as far as Buenos Aires to make Dita suspect him of cheating.

Damian returned to his suite and the phone was ringing. He hurried to answer it.

"Sir, I have an urgent matter that needs your attention," the hotel manager said.

Damian couldn't speak. He had a feeling Dita was in trouble.

"It's your wife, sir. There's been an accident."

Staff informed Damian that Dita had been found dead. Her body was discovered by the pool beneath the terrace. She could have fallen, staffers told him.

An investigation was underway. After the time of death and cause of death were determined, a homicide was suspected. Hotel staff verified his whereabouts in Buenos Aires, so Damian was ruled out as a potential suspect. His air-tight alibi coincided with suspicions of extra-marital relations in the marriage—evidence gathered from Dita's belongings, her phone, for example.

No allegations were made in connection to Damian. He was safe.

Damian did his best to cooperate. He shared whatever information he could except about Locrian, who was supposed to be out of town again.

Damian had to act quickly. His suspicions fell on Locrian, suspecting all along that Locrian had intended to meet her while he was gone. Locrian would be the subject of intense scrutiny. He had to capture him and do away with him while the police still had reason to believe that he'd gone into hiding.

Damian wanted revenge.

***

After the funeral service was completed, Damian set out to find Locrian, who had yet to be questioned by detectives assigned to the case. Locrian was toasting champagne with his friends at a restaurant on the night of the funeral. Damian consulted his many contacts and learned that Locrian would be at a popular bar on the Southside of Richmond the next Friday. Damian planned on walking up to him in the parking lot with a gun.

He staked out the bar that Friday night and waited for him outside. He immediately spotted him walking out the back door at close to midnight.

Locrian was driving a rental Ford, trying to look incognito.

"Hey, Loki," he called out from a distance, afraid Locrian would try something. He kept the gun in his coat pocket, ready for resistance.

"Hey, Damian. Sorry about Dita, ok? I didn't come to the funeral because I was busy."

"Too busy for old friends?" Damian answered, showcasing a grin.

"Well, unfortunately, business is business," Locrian said, eyeing the glove compartment of his rental, knowing it was a stretch to reach for it, suspecting that Damian harbored malicious intentions and that he had a weapon on him.

He wasn't stupid. Damian wouldn't have shown up for any other reason.

So, he played his card.

"I didn't come because I couldn't bear it. I loved Dita once, remember?"

"Business is business?" Damian seemed to ask. He would answer his question with one of his own—an obvious implication.

"Business or pleasure?"

Locrian knew. He had to get his gun, but Damian drew first. Locrian tried to play innocent, feigning shock at his friend's behavior.

"What are you doing?"

Damian opened the driver's seat of his Quattroporte.

"Get in the car!"

***

They drove to the cemetery where Dita was buried—none other than prestigious Hollywood Cemetery, burial place of affluent men and former statesmen. They found the mausoleum easily. It was one of the biggest and most costly of those erected there. But the mausoleum was in a corner lot overlooking the cliff sloping down to the James River, where tourists wouldn't possibly venture nearby.

Damian had plans for his beloved.

Locrian too. Damian ordered him to park the car at a walking distance from the mausoleum. They got out and looked at each other. One bled fear from his eyes while the other bred contempt. Damian asked his friend, "Why did you do it?"

"Do what?" Locrian replied.

"Take her from me."

"She didn't leave you, Damian. She didn't want to."

"You asked her?"

"Of course. I loved her!"

"You killed her!"

"I didn't!"

"Of course, you did."

"There were others! She had other lovers; I swear!"

"No! There weren't!"

"I'm telling the truth!"

"Don't lie to me!"

"I'm begging you!"

Tears fell from Locrian's eyes. Damian wouldn't have it. He ordered Locrian to go inside, so Locrian did.

"What are you doing?" Locrian cried. Damian was closing the door, locking it from the outside.

Passers-by wouldn't be able to hear the screams from inside the mausoleum.

***

Two weeks after Damian closed the doors of the mausoleum, he re-opened them. Locrian emerged from behind the tomb, shielding his arms from the bright, white light. His hands were caked with gore; it smudged his lips and stained his clothes. His large eyes were cold and plagued by jaundice. His fingers made gnarly and twisted gestures. He crawled closer and closer towards the entrance—no longer sane, no longer human, no longer the man Dita thought she could love on the side: charming, good-looking Locrian.

There wasn't much left of Dita's corpse. At first, Loki ate as little as he could. With the hunger pangs predicating the stomachache and diarrhea, he got used to the taste of rotten meat. Since she was eviscerated, eating the flesh became easier, without the internal organs adding to the spoilage.

Locrian shared the mausoleum with vermin and all sorts of insects. Damian showed an unbelievable level of tolerance to the stench. Locrian had bite marks, scabs, boils and bruises. Damian could barely believe his eyes. Locrian showed remarkable resilience, having stayed alive.

He had sunken so far down the food chain. Even coffin worms didn't live to be farmed.

He was on his haunches, looking at Damian, still shielding his eyes. Damian pointed his gun at him, smiling, satisfied with the carnage. A search was being conducted. Missing Persons reports had already been filed. They were offering a reward for anyone who could provide information on Locrian's whereabouts.

Locrian pleaded with his eyes. "Enough. Please. Enough." they seemed to say unintelligibly, like he had forgotten the words out of sheer barbarity.

Damian's eyes narrowed into slits. Gesturing at Locrian with his gun, he made him back up a few feet. Damian began closing the door of the mausoleum again.

Locrian went insane; he was disconsolate. He tore at his clothes, shrieking, wounding himself further as he pounded his arms against the pavement, knowing that staying another week would see him through to his death.

He lunged at Damian, but Damian fired a shot in the air and forced Locrian back. Locrian looked at him beseechingly. *Weren't we the best of friends once,* the look on his face seemed to say? *How can you?* His eyes begged for an answer. *How can you do this to me?*

Damian smiled like a man beyond compassion, loving the sight of Locrian Sumner's unspeakable suffering.

Locrian crouched behind a tomb in the dark. His eyes had adapted to seeing things move in the shadows. He had watched large rats infiltrate the mausoleum through fissures beneath the door and drainage ports. Once they smelled bloody carnage, there had been no stopping them. In the dark, they came in numbers. Having eaten what remained of Dita, Locrian would be next. He was food for the gods of the graveyard.

Damian envisioned Locrian choking Dita on the night of the murder. Damian believed that Locrian went to Dita that night to propose to her and was outraged when Dita tried to end the affair. Locrian had wanted her to divorce Damian so she could take half of his estate. Then Locrian and Dita would start a new life elsewhere.

And Damian believed that she wouldn't. She was torn by her loyalty to Damian and their shared moments of passion. Dita and Locrian argued. She asked him to leave the premises, then threatened to call the police. Locrian wasn't about to take no for an answer. He came up from behind her and she turned around. His hand caught her throat. He squeezed it until she felt limp and she resisted less and less. She fell off the balcony and lay next to the pool—a fool to think she could lead two lives at alternating moments, a fool to think she could trick both men into temptation's nest and still have it all.

Damian thought he knew better and he knew that he wasn't going to get caught. He drove back to his old home, to the scene of the murder, just to revisit the place where he had lost an old friend who was nothing more than a traitor; where he'd lost the woman he planned on spending the rest of his life with, nothing more than an unfaithful lover meeting an unsavory end. He later sold the place and moved to another part of the country to meet someone new.

There were others, Locrian had said. Damian refused to even remotely consider it. Merciless Damian, granting Locrian a suffering no person deserved to endure. Beyond reason, he continued to blame Locrian for Dita's murder, imagining the whole fantastical scenario of Locrian choking her after she'd refused him, even after the police would arrest the true killer in Dita's murder—a friend of hers—a nameless, mysterious lover Dita carelessly rendezvoused with, too. The man's DNA matched those on the bedsheets collected during the investigation, evidence that without a doubt proved Locrian was innocent of the crime.

My Brother's Keeper

Dorothy Davies

From church to home takes two thousand three hundred and forty one steps. I cross three roads, which means I step up and down six kerbs. I saw thirty two cars and four omnibuses. This day I saw no dogs. I did see forty seven seagulls and thirty two crows.

I saw seventeen people who were not in church. I saw twenty five people who were in church. I saw twenty four people who were not there for any real reason I could see. The preacher was the only person who seemed 'right' in my reasoning. I did not see myself in church, so I did not count myself as being in the congregation. I worried about this, should I have looked at myself in a mirror and counted myself as being there? Would the calculations be wrong?

Today the preacher spoke for ninety seven minutes and forty five seconds. I did not count his words. I feel a loss within myself that I did not do so but I was distracted by his sermon and my need to think about whether I should be included in the congregation count. I needed to resolve that in my mind.

The preacher spoke at length on the topic of 'Am I My Brother's Keeper?' He concluded that we were so, that we had a responsibility to take care of each other, no matter who we were and what we did.

I saw the twenty four people in church shifting in their pews and wondering how they could do this without putting any strain or effort on their mundane lives. I knew then I was right not to count myself among them.

I am my brother's keeper.

I have no need of wondering how I could do such a thing and not put a strain or effort on my mundane life. I wanted to tell the preacher when we left that I was a true keeper of my brother, but feared he would not understand.

So I walked the two thousand three hundred and forty one steps, crossed the three roads, navigating the six kerbs and finally arrived at my home.

I went down the sixteen steps to the cellar and walked the seventeen paces to where my brother languishes behind the bars of his cage.

I confirmed for myself again, yes, I am my brother's keeper.

If the preacher touches on that topic again, I'll tell him just how I fit into that category.

I'm sure he'll be impressed.

We All Feel Better In The Dark

Paul Edwards

Craig saw the For-Sale sign standing in the weed-strewn front garden of his parents' house. Once he was baptised, the hope and dream was for them all to live together in his grandfather's place. Granddad had been talking about starting and growing a church for years. Family values carefully shaped and distorted into an uncompromising new religion.

Craig knew he was next in line. Due his initiation tomorrow, in fact. But he had special plans all of his own and he fully intended on actioning them first.

He crossed the garden to the front door, clutching a large bunch of pink lilies. He knocked and Mum opened up with a confused expression on her face. "Craig! What a lovely surprise. Didn't expect to see you today." She stank of a sickly-sweet perfume over generously applied. "For me?" she said as he proffered the flowers. "What have I done to deserve these?"

Craig just smiled, saying nothing.

She waved him in, making her way along the hall toward the kitchen. "Can't believe tomorrow's your big day."

"Where's Dad?" he asked, ignoring her comment.

"Out in the garage. Tinkering on his car, as usual. I'll go fetch him, shall I?"

"No need. I'll go say hello in a bit."

She entered the kitchen, putting the flowers in the sink and turned her back on him as she began trimming the stalks.

"How's the flat?"

"Fine."

"Enjoying your independence?" She could barely disguise the disgust in her voice, which amused him greatly.

"Sure." He stuck his hand into his pocket, stroking and feeling the leather strap. He'd sneaked it out of his parents' wardrobe years ago and kept it with him ever since. Originally it was to stop her from using it on him.

"Does Dad still have his old pistol upstairs?"

She cocked her head slightly. "Why on earth would you ask that?"

"Just remember seeing it as a kid, that's all."

She returned to the task of trimming the flowers. "I suppose it's up there somewhere."

He drew the strap out of his pocket, then moved quickly behind her, slipping it around her neck, hearing a series of animalistic grunts and snorts escape her. She squirmed and struggled against him, repeatedly kicking the cabinet door. Finally, she stopped fighting. He untangled the strap and watched her slump heavily to the floor.

He kicked her…

…*and saw himself down there, hands raised, yelling, crying out as Mum beat him with the strap, her fleshy face flushed, livid and contorted.*

"How dare *you call my father that!"* she screamed. *"How* dare *you! How dare you speak about your grandfather that way!"*

Craig wandered out into the garden, spying Dad inside his garage, bent over the front of his grey Morris Minor. An assortment of car parts and tools lay scattered around his feet.

Craig stooped, snatching up a claw hammer.

Had Dad always been so quick to accept Mum's family, he wondered? Perhaps he had been propelled by demons of his own; after all, they say like attracts like.

Craig moved swiftly, keenly, behind him, raising the hammer before driving it down hard onto the back of his father's head. Dad staggered forward, groaning, flailing his arms. Craig landed further blows, one after the other, beating his father mercilessly to the ground.

There was blood in Craig's eyes; he had to wipe it away to see:

...himself back inside the house, considerably younger, smaller. He was dressed in pyjamas and slippers; his father had seen him up and about using the bathroom only moments before and was now calling for him from inside his parents' bedroom.

Craig shuffled slowly into the room, then froze – sick to the very bottom of his stomach at the sight before him.

"Close the door," his father instructed. *"Go stand in the corner. Watch. Do as I say. Under this roof, we hide nothing from each other."*

199

He did as he was told, staring at the naked forms on the bed, moving, twisting, fusing.

Skin pressing against skin.

Laughter.

Whispers.

Pants, groans.

Two as one.

A meld of glistening flesh...

***

It was late. Close to midnight. A full moon hovered spectrally over the roofs of the housing estate. Craig sat in contemplative silence, allowing a succession of memories to flood him. Of setting up armies of toy soldiers in his and his brother's room, despite Andy being a little too old for the game. Trading jokes and whispering to each other after lights out. Andy sharing a cigarette with him outside the school gates when he was fourteen.

He quickly rubbed his eyes, the memories dissipating instantly.

He grabbed a canister in the footwell, then clambered out of the car. Closed the driver's-side door and pulled the hood of his jacket up over his head. He crossed the road, avoiding the streetlamp's glow. The windows of his brother's house were smothered with darkness; there was no sign of anyone up. Petrol syphoned from Dad's Morris Minor sloshed around inside the canister.

He paused, glancing up and down the street. Good, he thought: *no one around*. He stared at the living room window, seeing his own pale face float in that small square of blackness.

Andy lived with his two boys, Sam, aged 6 and Jonathan, aged 5. Andy was a fair few years older than Craig, but they'd always been close. Until Andy got baptised, of course.

Craig hurriedly twisted off the top of the canister, spreading the petrol around inside the porch and then splashing it up the walls. He lit a match, threw it. Turned and ran for cover.

He reached his car, leapt inside. Pulled the door closed and slunk down, hearing the flames outside roar.

The street suddenly lit up, people out shouting and screaming...

...but Craig was sat on a bench with Andy in the park, watching Jonathan and Sam play together on a climbing frame.

Andy was smiling at him. "I'm honestly doing okay," he said. "I don't think about Marie at all now. I've come to realise that she wasn't the one. She wouldn't accept us. Any of us. And family's important, right?"

Craig said nothing, his hands thrust deep into the pockets of his jacket.

"I still have the boys. She was never going to take them away from me."

Craig remained silent, mulling this over for a moment.

"What are you thinking?" Andy asked.

Craig shrugged. Then, very softly, quietly, he said: "What happens down there, Andy?"

Andy turned away, watching his kids charge around the climbing frame. Then, turning back, meeting Craig's gaze again, he shrugged and replied, "They lock you down there and the darkness just fills you up. That's all there is to it."

"What is it that's down there, Andy?"

"It needs us," Andy said, ignoring the question, urgency building in his voice. "Then we need it. We all feel better in the dark, Craig."

Craig looked toward Andy's children on the climbing frame.

He was shaking like a leaf now.

"Your boys," he whispered. "Will you let the same thing happen to them?"

***

Craig arrived at the base of the hill just after sunrise. He got out of the car, thrust his hood up, and climbed the hill.

Granddad's place awaited him at the top, looking almost serene under the slats of early morning sunlight. There was scaffolding up and land cleared away around it, all ready for the extension.

The front door was unlocked. Craig pushed on through, entering the hall. The stairs faced him, leading up to a deserted landing. To his right, open space: Granddad's large sitting room. Craig reached into his jacket pocket, touching and stroking metal.

Granddad was sitting in his armchair, his back to Craig. He was an early riser; awake with the sparrow's fart, as he used to say.

Craig waited a few contemplative seconds, telling himself *I can finish this*. Then, breathing out quietly, slowly, he wandered across into his grandfather's line of sight and flicked off the TV.

"Who...?" Granddad began, jolting, sitting bolt upright in his seat.

The outraged expression on Granddad's face softened. "Craig?"

"Hi, Granddad."

Craig grabbed a stool by the TV, sitting himself on it. Stared his grandfather hard in the eye. *I'm not afraid of you anymore,* he thought.

"What are you doing here?"

"Thought I'd come early." Craig managed to project a smile. "It's my big day, remember? My eighteenth birthday. The time when I'm finally supposed to accept all this, right?"

Granddad nodded vaguely, his eyes betraying his suspicion. "Your parents here?"

Craig shook his head.

Granddad threw a glance at the door beneath the stairs.

Craig looked, too. Then, reaching deep inside his jacket pocket, he carefully extracted Dad's pistol.

"Craig..." Granddad began, waving his hand vigorously in the air.

Craig cocked the gun, pointing it directly at the old man.

"Craig," Granddad said again, showing him his palms in what appeared to be a gesture of utter desperation. "It's *all* good, okay? Once it's done, you'll realise. You'll *see*. Just… just understand that…"

"Bye."

A bullet tore right through Granddad's face, knocking the old man back into his chair, his body slowly sliding down the seat to flop brokenly over the armrest. A thread of smoke coiled lazily up to the ceiling from the crown of Granddad's head. Craig stood up and put three more bullets into him.

He lowered his arm, puffed out his cheeks. Looked about…

…and saw his family congregated around him inside this very room. But there was someone missing – and very quickly he turned toward the cellar door.

Andy.

The door was shut tight.

Mum and Dad were sitting on the sofa, hand-in-hand, their expressions one of strange joy and pride. Granddad had his hands on Craig, his long, nicotine-stained fingers gripping and kneading Craig's arms.

Andy was kicking and punching the cellar door, screaming at the top of his lungs.

"It comes part and parcel with being a member of this family," Granddad explained. "We accept it because of the love we share and the traditions we carry."

Craig wanted to wriggle free and help his brother, but Grandad held him hard and fast and wouldn't let go.

"It's what being a family's about. All things suffered and shared, young man. And that," he

nodded at the cellar door, "is what binds us all together."

Craig blinked back into the present moment.

He sat down again on the stool, gazing at the twisted, curled-up form of his grandfather. He closed his eyes and heard a soft *click* come from the other side of the room. He opened his eyes, looked across the room at the cellar door.

It was standing open now, revealing flickering, unfolding strands of a strange and sentient darkness.

If he wasn't going in, he realised, then it was going to have to come out for him.

He watched the darkness invade the room, weaving and coiling into the air, shimmering before him like a heat haze. He felt it wind itself around him, pressing up close, emitting a series of eerie whistling and howling sounds. He could see it clearer now, a little better – snake-like, vapor-like, consisting of swirling black wisps, tendrils, and tongues.

Craig slammed shut his eyes.

Let it in some, he thought. *Just enough, and...*

His fingers tightened around Dad's pistol.

The darkness was infiltrating him now, passing through his mouth and nostrils, corrupting him and all that he could ever be. He felt it fight against his intense revulsion, trying, cannily, to normalise itself within him.

He wasn't going to let that happen.

He lifted the gun and pressed its muzzle tight against his temple. Seconds later he squeezed the trigger, purifying the darkness, purging it with fleeting, searing light, consigning his family's twisted secrets and traditions to the oblivion they deserved.

The Curse of Repetitive Circles

David Turnbull

Something didn't feel right.

For a start there was that strange beeping noise that kept stopping and starting. And the weird thought in his head that accompanied the noise every time he heard it. *That sounds like a mobile phone. But mobile phones haven't been invented yet.*

What was that noise?

More to the point, what was a mobile phone and how did he come to know about them if they hadn't been invented? It was a strange day all round. It felt like a repetition of events that had already happened.

Kevin walked over to his model train set. It was laid out on the old wallpaper trellis his dad had let him use. He was proud of what he'd created. The station with its scale model passengers waiting on the platform. The bridge that spanned the track. The red postal van crossing the bridge. The little woodland area beyond the bridge with its cluster of synthetic trees sprouting from a flat patch of green felt grass. The girl on the white horse raising her arm to wave as the train went past.

How the track looped up a little incline and back to station.

Good job, Kevin.

That's what his dad said when he saw the finished results.

Kevin turned the key at the side of the engine and set it running around the circular track, pulling its two carriages behind it. Off it went, out of the station, under the bridge, past the woods. The girl on the white horse waved. Up the incline it huffed and back to station, rattling past the platform where the little plastic commuters were cursed to eternally wait and never board.

Something wasn't right. He was positive he'd done this exact thing before. Stood on this exact spot. Watched the train go round the track. It was like a repetition. Of course, I've done this before, he assured himself. A zillion times. It's my train set. I play with it all the time. Of course, I've stood on this exact spot. Where else would I stand?

But he'd never heard that beeping noise before.

He couldn't figure out where it was coming from.

It sounds like a mobile phone, he thought. *But it can't be. Mobile phones haven't been invented yet.*

There was an odd smell in the air, acrid and smoky. It stung his eyes a little. He wondered if the neighbours were burning weeds in their garden. There was a muffled sound too. Like a voice saying something which couldn't quite be made out. It seemed be coming from above the ceiling. He wondered if his dad had come home early from work and had gone into the attic to tidy up.

On the wall above the model station, he'd turned the lid of the train set into a kind of poster. It showed a boy in school uniform kneeling down before the engine and carriages. *Hornby Trains* it read in big block letters. And then in smaller letters beneath - *clockwork*. And then in even smaller letters - *British and Guaranteed*. And in a rectangle border to the bottom right- *manufactured by Meccano Ltd, Binns Road, Liverpool, 13.*

As he looked at it, Kevin felt an odd little twitch in his ears. As if he was expecting to hear something at any moment. Not the beeping. He was expecting that, but there was something else. Something that should happen right about now. There it was, right on cue. The theme song from the Casey Jones television series, drifting upstairs from the front room.

Something surely wasn't right.

This exact thing had definitely happened before.

Without fully understanding how he'd gotten downstairs, he found himself in the armchair in front of a square shaped black and white TV set. The Casey Jones theme song boomed from the set's single amplifier. On the screen the Cannonball Express was hurtling along the track, steaming and rolling, gushing black smoke from its funnel, Casey at the throttle. The actors and their names appeared on the screen. Alan Hale as Casey Jones. Bobby Clarke as Casey Jnr. Dub Taylor as Wallie Sims and Eddie Waller as Red Rock. Finally, Mary Wallace as Alice Jones.

The episode opened with an explosion in a mineshaft and the excavation crew getting trapped inside. I know this, thought Kevin; I've seen this episode before. I know exactly what's going to happen. It's going to be Casey and the Cannonball to the rescue.

There it was again, that unsettling feeling that things were repeating over and over.

Something else wasn't quite right. Something was missing. His sister. Where was Ruthie? By now she should be seated at the dining table, diligently doing her homework. Where could she be at this time? It wasn't like her to get a detention or anything.

Give it till the end of Casey Jones, he told himself. Then go out and look for her.

Mum would be home soon. Her overalls would waft the vanilla essence of the biscuit factory. Half an hour or so later Dad would arrive, all neat and tidy in his uniform from the station ticket office. He better make sure he found Ruthie before they arrived. You're the oldest, they'd scold him. You're supposed to be the responsible one.

Maybe Dad was already home?

Maybe he was up in the attic?

Maybe Ruthie was up there with him?

That might explain the muffled voices.

The episode of Casey Jones seemed so familiar. I've seen this before, he thought. More than once. He wondered if Mum had left a note for him on kitchen counter with instructions for tea. She often did that. Like, *there's a meat pie in the oven, switch it on at medium.* Or, *boil the potatoes in the pot.*

He should go to the kitchen and look but he felt oddly compelled to stick with Casey Jones, even if he'd seen the episode before. It was drawing to a conclusion now anyway. Casey had saved the miners and saved the day.

The closing version of the Casey Jones song filled the room.

So long for now we'll be seeing you when / Casey comes a rolling by again.

I'll go and see if there's a note in the kitchen, he told himself. Then I'll go and look in the attic. If no one is up there, I'll go and look for Ruthie.

But as soon as he stepped through the door that led to the kitchen, he found himself inexplicably back in his bedroom. The model train was still running around the track. Under the bridge, past woodland and the girl waving from the white horse. Up the incline and past the passengers on the platform. Then round it went again.

This is impossible, he thought. The clockwork mechanism should have run out of momentum ages ago. It's like I'm on that train. Going round and round and seeing the exact same things over and over. The girl on the white horse never lowers her arms. The red postal van is always at the same spot on the bridge.

Then came that sound.

Beep-beep. Beep-beep.

And Kevin thought it sounded like a mobile phone.

And then he told himself it wasn't possible because they hadn't been invented yet.

On the dresser the lid of his Dansette record player sat open. There was a 45rpm record on the central spindle. He clicked the switch. The turntable began to spin. The record dropped down. The arm juddered sideways. Before the needle touched the groove on the vinyl, he knew with an unsettling certainty that the song would be Morning Town Ride by The Seekers.

Train whistle blowing, sang Judith Durham.

Kevin lay down on the bed. He felt queasy and disorientated. There were still muffled sounds coming from above. He picked up the book that lay on the bedside table. Murder on the Orient Express by Agatha Christie.

Judith Durham was singing about the sandman swinging a lantern to show that all was well. I really should go and see where Ruthie has gotten to, he told himself. Instead, he flipped open the book and tried to focus on Hercule Poirot's crime solving deductions as his train hurtled toward Stamboul. The smell of smoke grew stronger. His eyes stung.

Beep-beep, went the strange noise.

He felt he should get up and check in case something was burning in the oven. He should go look for his sister. She should be home from school by now. But he felt so weary. The words on the page were beginning to blur and his eyelids were getting heavy.

***

The dream he dreamt seemed somehow more real than the loop he felt trapped in.

He was travelling on a train from London Bridge to Sidcup. He had no idea why he was going to Sidcup. He'd never heard of the place. He had no clue as to where it was. The train pulled out of its stop at a station called Hither Green. Again, he had no idea where that was. He reached into his pocket and fetched a Kit Kat. He peeled back the foil, snapped off a finger and bit through the chocolate to the wafer, then opened the newspaper that sat on his lap.

His body felt odd. Bigger and taller. His knees and elbows and finger joints ached.

The words on the page swirled. He couldn't make head or tail of them. He popped the remaining half of the Kit Kat finger into his mouth. As he crunched through the chocolate to the wafer beneath there came an ear-splitting screech of carriage wheels against iron rails. A shower of yellow sparks arced past the window. The train tipped to one side so violently that he was thrown from his seat.

The carriage went into a tumble as it rolled down an embankment. His back hit the ceiling with an agonising thump. He heard screams and cries as the other passengers were scattered and tossed like rag dolls. Glass shattered. Wood splintered. Metal buckled. He bounced back onto a chair and fell into the aisle, hearing the snap of bones.

A moment of utter darkness.

Then the sensation of something pinning him in place, crushing agonisingly down on him. The groan of metal straining against metal. Swirls of smoke, burning his throat and lungs. A shape taking form in the darkness. Something moving. Something slow and serpentine, swathed in shadow.

213

It rose before him, settling into the hunched shape of a man.

"Hurry along, old boy. We're all bound for Morning Town. Many miles to go."

The voice was like dried autumn leaves crushed against frost coated gravel. The breath that hushed out with the words reeked like old chunks of beef left to sweat in the sun. Kevin felt the gooseflesh pop all over him like a chicken pox rash. He shivered as a tremble seized him from head to toe.

And the terrible face that grinned down at him was emaciated, almost skeletal. Brown wizened flesh stretched back to the contours of the skull, creviced and scuffed like old leather. The man was dressed like a train guard but instead of railway logo on the badge above the peak of his cap, there was a skull and cross bones.

The hideous face beneath the cap regarded him through darkly sunken eyes. A nightmare grin curved on blackened lips. The mouth was filled with teeth that were unevenly set, listing like gravestones littering some ancient graveyard. His uniform was mildewed and dusty. He held up a clipboard in a skeletal hand that was as curved as the scimitar claw of a hawk.

"Kevin Ellis," he said. *"Your name is on my manifest. Hurry on board. There's not a second to waste."*

A black centipede came wriggling out of the dark slit of one nostril and curved its way back into the dark slit of the other. Kevin screamed and found himself suddenly wide awake and standing back in front of his model railway set.

***

And so it went again from the start.

Beep-beep came the strange noise.

He couldn't tell where it was coming from.

But it sounded like a mobile phone.

Only it couldn't be.

Such things hadn't been invented yet.

Kevin wound the key and set the train on the track. It pulled away from the model station with its little plastic passengers on the platform, who never got a chance to board. Under the bridge where the red postal van sat and never quite crossed. Past the copse of synthetic trees impaled in the little green patch of felt grass. Past the girl on the white horse whose arm was raised and frozen mid wave. Up the incline and past the station, not stopping for passengers.

And there was a smell of smoke that made his eyes smart. And a sound like someone talking above him in the attic. And he looked at the Hornby box lid pinned to the wall. And the train went round and round on the track and never seemed to run out of steam.

And right on cue there came the opening lines of the Casey Jones theme song. And he was somehow in the armchair in front of the TV set. The credits were running. The Cannonball Express was steaming and rolling. There was a cave in at the mine. He'd seen this episode before.

215

He wondered where his sister was. It wasn't like Ruthie not to be home yet. She liked to get her homework done. First thing she'd do once she took off her coat was set out her homework on the table and get stuck into it. Kevin could watch whatever he wanted on TV, so long as he left her in peace to get her homework done.

He really should go and look for her.

He wondered if there was a note on the kitchen table. Was there something in the oven? Or a pot of potatoes on the stove, waiting to be boiled. He wondered if his mum's overalls would deliciously waft vanilla when she arrived home. He wondered if his dad was up in the attic. He wondered if Ruthie was up there with him.

And then he was back in his room and the train was still making circuits around the track. And the lid of the Dansette was open. And the record dropped to the turntable. And the needle dropped to the record. And Judith Durham sang about the driver at the engine and the fireman ringing the bell.

He lay down on his bed and picked up the book from his bedside table. Murder on the Orient Express. He was curious to know what progress Poirot was making in his investigations. The words on the page seemed familiar. He really should go and see where Ruthie was. But his eyes felt heavy, and his head felt drowsy.

***

"Where have you been, old boy?" demanded the skeletal guard who'd wormed his way back into

Kevin's dream once more. *"All the other passengers are waiting. We're building up a head of steam. Any minute now that old whistle is going to blow. Whoo! Whoo! All aboard!"*

Kevin could feel that terrible pressure pressing down on him again. He couldn't move. The smoke was stinging his eyes. It was getting harder and harder to breathe. Every time he sucked in air the smoke burned his lungs. The wreck of the carriage creaked and groaned all around him.

He thought he heard that muffled voice coming from somewhere above his head.

"Look lively, old boy," interrupted the guard. *"Your name is on my manifest. Your seat is booked and ready."*

"I didn't book any seat," said Kevin.

"All done for you," said the guard and showed his gravestone teeth as he grinned his crooked grin. *"This is the mystery train. The last train to Clarksville. The Marrakech Express. The train they call the City of New Orleans. Call it what you will. We might be gone five thousand miles when this day is done. And five thousand more before the dawn. We might go right on into infinity. All you've got to do, old boy, is take my hand and I'll haul you aboard."*

He reached out his long, bony, skeletal hand.

It crept toward Kevin like a scuttling sun-bleached crab.

Kevin screamed and recoiled.

***

Beep-beep went the strange noise.

It sounded like a mobile phone.

But that was impossible.

In a way it was comforting, this endlessly going round in circles. Reliving the same scenarios time and time again. The model railway watched over by its box lid poster. The bridge, the red postal van, the waving girl on her white horse, the passengers waiting on the platform. The opening credits to Casey Jones. The episode with a cave in at the mine. The needle dropping to the record. The familiar song. Judith Durham's voice. The book. Agatha Christie, Murder on the Orient Express.

Nothing unexpected. Nothing unpredictable.

A place for everything. Everything in its place.

But on the other hand, this endless predictability felt claustrophobic and suffocating. You just had to go round and endlessly round. Same old same old. And your stomach was full dread. Your sister hadn't come home from school. You couldn't go look for her because you were compelled to complete the circuit of the endless loop.

And you knew, you just knew, with a stone-cold certainty that coated your heart in a thick casing of ice, exactly where the route was taking you next. And who you were going to see when you got there. And what he was going to want you to do.

***

"Damn it, old boy," said the guard. *"Would you stop wandering off? Everyone is waiting and you're procrastinating."*

The carriage groaned. Kevin felt the pressure that clamped him in place tighten. Something had moved. Moved in a bad way. A way that might have terrible consequences. There was a sharp pain in his lungs now. More than just the burn of the smoke that got sucked in every time he drew breath.

"Who's waiting?" he managed to ask.

The guard grinned and stared back intently through his darkly, sunken eyes.

"All of them," he replied. *"All of the ones who boarded at London Bridge and New Cross and Lewisham and Hither Green. All the ones who'll never get off this train, but will board my train instead. All of them waiting for an inconsiderate old man who won't accept he's on the manifest."*

"I'm not an old man," said Kevin. "You've got the wrong person. Maybe this old man has the same name as me?"

The guard laughed and his leathery skin stretched taut across his hollow cheeks.

"There's no mistake, old boy. If your name is on my manifest, you're bound for Morning Town – no doubt about it. There are others waiting for you there, you know. Waiting on the platform to greet you when you step down from the train."

"Who?" demanded Kevin. "Who would be waiting for me in such a place?"

The guard leaned in close. Kevin found himself again engulfed in a putrid fug of meaty breath. *"Your parents,"* said the guard. *"Grandparents*

219

from both sides of your family. Your cousin Pete, who died of a ruptured appendix. Your mother's uncle George. Wounded and drowned before he set a single foot on that fateful beach in Normandy. They'll all come to greet you. And, your wife will be there and she'll be smiling sweetly."

"My parents are not dead," said Kevin. "They just haven't come home from work yet. And I definitely don't have a wife."

"They boarded my train long ago," insisted the guard. *"They're waiting for you. All you have to do is step on-board."*

"Lair!" yelled Kevin.

He heard the muffled sound above him again.

It was becoming a little more distinct.

He thought it sounded like a man's voice.

"Just take my hand, damn it," interrupted the guard. *"Take my hand and I'll haul you on board. I'll show you to your seat. Reserved specifically for you. I'll put a big fat tick next to your name on the manifest and we'll be off at last."*

"I can't," said Kevin. "My sister is missing. I have to find her."

"You're the one who's missing," said the guard.

***

Kevin watched his model train make another circuit of the track. Any minute now the theme tune to Casey Jones would start. He thought about what the guard had told him in his dream.

220

It sure would be nice to see his grandparents again. From when he was the age of five onward, they'd died one by one. One after the other. Falling like dominoes, his father had said. Kevin thought that was so unfair. Most of his school friends had grandparents who were still alive.

His grandmother could make cheese scones that just about melted in your mouth. His father's parents had a little farm, with a tractor and a hayloft and a duck pond and everything.

And how about his cousin Pete? He'd been a year older than Kevin. When he was alive, he used to come at the weekends. They'd ride their bikes from sunrise to sunset. Kevin missed all that. It would be so great to see Pete again.

Then there was George. His grandmother's dear departed brother, who Kevin had never even met. George who looked so handsome in his uniform in the framed picture that sat on the mantel. I bet you anything he goes around Morning Town dressed in that uniform, Kevin told himself.

The whole family would be reunited.

Only it wouldn't be the whole family. His parents wouldn't be there. The guard was lying about that. His sister wouldn't be there. She was missing. She hadn't come home from school. He should really go and look for her.

From downstairs he heard the Casey Jones theme starting.

*Stop and listen because you're going to hear /
a brand new story about a great engineer.*

***

"You're a slippery one," said the guard, once he was back in the dream. *"Always off somewhere else when you should already be in your seat."*

"Go without me, then," said Kevin, feeling the pressure crushing in on him.

"Your name is on my manifest," snapped the guard. *"I couldn't contemplate leaving without you."*

Beep-beep went the noise.

It sounded like a mobile phone.

When he looked there was something in his hand. A black oblong shape with a glass screen. *Beep-beep* it went, as if demanding to be answered. A name was flashing on the screen.

Ruth, it flashed.

Ruthie? thought Kevin.

And somehow, he knew which button to press and then to hold the oblong contraption to his ear. "Kevin?" said the voice on the other side. "Kevin, is that you? I was waiting at Sidcup station, just like we agreed. There was an announcement about the derailment. I've been so worried."

"Ruthie?" he said back. "Is that you?"

"Ruthie?" said the voice. "You haven't called me that for years. Not since we were kids."

"Where are you?" he demanded. "You should have been home from school ages ago. I was about to come and look for you. Mum and Dad are going to be furious."

"Mum and Dad? What on earth are you talking about? Mum passed on ten years ago. Nearly twenty since Dad died. Are you hurt, Kevin? Did you get hurt in the train crash? Are you concussed? Is someone looking after you?"

So many questions.

Kevin didn't know what to say.

The contraption at his ear juddered once and the voice on the other side fell silent.

"Battery died, old boy," chuckled the guard. *"Yours is about to go too. So get yourself on my train, pronto. Before the last bar blinks out."*

Kevin heard the muffled sounds from above his head again. Focus, he told himself. Listen. Try to hear what's being said. He closed his eyes and strained to hear. And like magic the voice became a male voice, loud and baritone, addressing him directly.

"Hey, Mister. Mister, can you hear me? Look up at me if you can hear me."

He found himself bathed in a wedge of bright light.

He managed somehow to strain his neck so he could look up. A face was gazing down at him through a gap in the mangled wreckage. He was wearing a fireman's helmet. The light was emanating from a torch mounted on the brim.

"You hear me, Mister?" asked the fireman. "You see me?"

Kevin opened his mouth to reply. It felt dry. His teeth had the coppery tang of blood on them. "Yes," he managed to croak. "I see you."

The fireman disappeared for a moment. "Over here!" Kevin heard him yell. "There's a live one over here. Old guy. Late sixties. Bring the cutting gear!"

Then the shrill sound of a whistle being blown.

Late sixties? Though Kevin. *How can that be? When did that happen?*

The fireman reappeared in the mouth of the ragged gap.

"You hold on, Mister," he said. "Don't go drifting off to sleep. We'll have you out of there soon. Just stay with me. Can you do that?"

"I don't know," replied Kevin. "I'm feeling pretty damned tired."

The fireman removed his glove and stretched his arm down into the belly of the wreck.

"Just hold on to my hand, Mister. My friends are coming. I swear we'll get you out."

The stench of rotting meat heralded the guard materialising out of the smoky darkness once more. Wizened skin and sunken eyes, crooked gravestone grin. *"Don't you dare take his hand, old boy. Take mine. Your seat is waiting for you. We're running late."*

And the skeletal hand came scuttling like a crab again.

One hand or the other?

It was a life of death decision. Above him a hand that would pull him into the daylight. Below him a hand that would drag him into the darkness. One hand representing life. The other hand representing the afterlife.

The choice should be obvious.

Choose life.

Reach up and take the fireman's hand.

But reality was crashing in on him.

He'd been sixty-eight last May. His parents had died years ago. His wife had died six months ago, a broken woman. He had two sons. Neither of them had contacted him since the funeral. Hardly surprising. He'd been a terrible husband and father. A philander and a compulsive gambler. His punishment was debilitating loneliness. All he had to look forward to was a trip once a month to visit his ever tolerant sister, who lived in Sidcup.

Did he really want to go back to all of that? Would it not be better to call it quits now? Make the transfer. Go with the guard? Ride the train to Morning Town? Reunite with his family? See his wife again? Beg forgiveness for all his indiscretions.

But could he trust the guard?

We might go right on into infinity. Hadn't he said those exact words?

What to do?

Decisions, decisions.

"Mister," called the fireman. "Don't close your eyes. Stay with me."

"Don't you go wandering off again, old boy," warned the guard. *"This is your last chance. Take my hand now, or I leave without you."*

One hand or the other?

He needed time to think.

He knew where he should go.

Somewhere that time seemed frozen.

***

225

Kevin wound the key and set the train on the track. It pulled away from the model station with its little plastic passengers on the platform. Under the bridge where the red postal van sat. Past the copse of trees impaled in the green felt grass. Past the girl on the white horse, whose raised arm was frozen mid wave. Up the incline.

He looked up at the Hornby box lid pinned to the wall. And the train went round and round on the track and never seemed to run out of steam. Soon he'd be in the armchair in front of the TV set. The credits would run. The Cannonball Express, steaming and rolling. A cave in at the mine.

Then back in his room. The needle would drop to the record. Judith Durham would sing about a train whistle blowing. He'd pick up the copy of Murder on the Orient Express and he'd read the same page. The sentences and paragraphs he knew by heart.

But it was different now.

There was no odd beeping noise. No smoke smarting at his eyes. No sound of muffled voices from above. He didn't wonder if there was a note left in the kitchen, or where his sister was, or when his parents would be home. There would be no skeletal hand creeping toward him like a crab. No wizened old guard with a promise of some mythical faraway place.

With a crushing predictability the theme song from Casey Jones drifted up from downstairs. He knew the plot of the episode by heart. He could recite the dialogue line for line. The monotony wrapped lead around his weary bones. His shoulders slumped. Round and around he went. Again and again and again.

The dragging of time had made him fully conscious of his circumstance. An old man in a child's body. He'd squandered his right to make a decision. Chosen a coward's retreat to the deceptive comfort of this nostalgic fragment. Life was a journey, whose ultimate destination was death. The journey after death might continue to who knew where. But the nightmare of purgatory was a curse of repetitive circles.

The horror gnawed like a rat at his soul.

Meet The Authors

Diane Arrelle has more than 350 short stories published and two short story collections: Just A Drop In The Cup and Seasons On The Dark Side. She, her sane husband and insane cat live on the edge of the New Jersey (USA) Pine Barrens (home of the Jersey Devil).

www.arrellewrites.com   FaceBook: Diane Arrelle

Neil Baker's other stories can be read in various publications from Dark Regions, Chaosium and Golden Goblin. He is also the founder of April Moon Books. By day he is a high school teacher, by night he dreams of Hammer films and rubber monsters. Neil is originally from the UK, but now lives with his family in Canada.

John Cady was born and raised in Southeastern Massachusetts. For the past thirteen years, he has taught the English Language Arts to incarcerated youth. When he's not teaching and making memories with his family, he is writing. His stories have been included in multiple horror anthologies including After The Kool Aid Is Gone, The Killer Collection, Flashes of Hope, and The ABC's of Terror Vol. 3.

Dorothy Davies is an editor, writer, photographer and medium. Somehow all these things come together in her seemingly crowded leisure and work life. She is an avid kindle user and delights in writing reviews for Amazon, especially when a novel is deleted a mere 2-3 chapters in and is too badly written to be read... she retired from editing for a while to run a second hand shop, the best one on the Isle of Wight, but the thrill of finding and publishing outstanding stories became too much so she started again with the Gravestone Press imprint. She still runs the shop...

R.G. Evans is the author of the poetry books *Overtipping the Ferryman, The Holy Both,* and *Imagine Sisyphus Happy,* as well as the horror novella *The Noise of Wings.* His poems, fiction and nonfiction, have appeared in *SurVision* (Ireland), *Rattle,* and *Weird Tales* among other publications. His collection of original songs, *Sweet Old LIfe,* is available on most streaming platforms. Recently retired after thirty-four years of high school teaching, Evans teaches creative writing at Rowan University in New Jersey, USA. Website: www.rgevanswriter.com

Paul Edwards is a life-long horror fan and writes his own twisted tales in any spare time that he can grab. He has seen three collections of stories published – *Now That I've Lost You* (Screaming Dreams), *Black Mirrors* (Rainfall Books) and *Night Voices* (Demain Publishing), the latter being a joint-collection with author Frank Duffy. Paul is also a fan of role-playing games, rock music and rough Somerset cider.

Michael B Fletcher is an Australian writer of adult and YA speculative fiction including fantasy, science fiction and horror. His first book *Kings of Under-Castle*, a series of humorous adventures featuring two rogues who live in the drains under a castle, was published by *IFWG Publishing Australia* in 2013.

Fletcher has over eighty short stories in magazines and anthologies in Australia, USA and the UK.

The first book of his fantasy trilogy, *Masters of Scent* is to be released by *IFWG Publishing Australia* in late 2022.

Fletcher has co-authored *Kat,* a YA Science Fiction currently being assessed for potential publication while *Mont of Siroc,* a YA Fantasy book is yet to be submitted.

Leslie Gulvas is a collector of experiences, a retired science teacher and a former research scientist. She lives on a little farm with a giant wolfhound and a disgruntled guard pig. Her writing features average people in extraordinary situations. Writing as Skeeter Enright, she has an urban fantasy novel, CARNIVAL CHARLATAN, and a Native American thriller OFF THE RESERVATION written as Lee Gull. Under her own name, she has over twenty published creative nonfiction articles and a children's picture book IGGY THE CONFUSED PIGGY. Her websites are: https://leegull.weebly.com and https://skeeterenright.weebly.com

Lena Ng

Lena Ng roams the dimensions Toronto, Ontario, and is a monster-hunting member of the Horror Writers Association. She has curiosities published in sixty tomes including *Amazing Stories* and the anthology *We Shall Be Monsters*, which was a finalist for the 2019 Prix Aurora Award. *Under an Autumn Moon* is her short story collection. She is currently seeking a publisher for her novel, *Darkness Beckons*, a Gothic romance.

SJ Townend hopes that her stories take the reader on a journey to often a dark place and only sometimes back again.

SJ won the Secret Attic short story contest (Spring 2020), has had fiction published with Sledgehammer Lit Mag, Hash Journal, Ghost Orchid Press, Bandit Fiction, Black Hare Press, Black Petals Horror Magazine, Ellipsis Zine, Gravely Unusual, Gravestone Press, Holy Flea, Horla Horror, and was long listed for the Women on Writing non-fiction contest in 2020.

She has also written and self-published two dark mystery novels, both of which are available to purchase on Amazon: (Tabitha Fox Never Knocks, Twenty-Seven and the Unkindness of Crows).

Follow her on Twitter: @SJTownend

Mark Towse is an Englishman living in Australia. He would sell his soul to the devil or anyone buying if it meant he could write full-time. Alas, he left it very late to begin this journey, penning his first story since primary school at the ripe old age of forty-five. Since then, he's been published in the likes of Flash Fiction Magazine, The Dread Machine, Cosmic Horror, Midnight in the Pentagram, Suspense Magazine, ParABnormal, and Raconteur. His work has also appeared on many exceptional podcasts such as The Grey Rooms, No Sleep, Creepy, Tales to Terrify, etc. His first collection, 'Face the Music,' was released by All Things That Matter Press in 2020. 'Nana,' his debut novella, was published by D&T Publishing in March 2021, available via the usual outlets.

David Turnbull is a member of the Clockhouse London group of genre writers. He writes mainly short fiction and has had numerous short stories published in magazines and anthologies. His stories have previously been featured at Liars League London events and read at other live events such as Solstice Shorts and Virtual Futures. He was born in Scotland, but now lives in the Catford area of London. He can be found at **www.tumsh.co.uk.**

Alaric Cabiling is an author and producer living in Manila, Philippines. He resided in Richmond, Virginia, United States, for seventeen years and much of his work takes place there. Ukiyoto Publishing House recently published his collection of stories, Il Migliore Del Mondo & Other Stories on June 2, 2021. He is disabled and identifies as gay.

Stuart Holland is the owner of Fiction4All, a golf enthusiast (especially the 19th hole) and has written in the genres of crime/mystery, thrillers and suspense, and has now turned his hand to horror. His books are available from fiction4all.com in both digital and print editions. His other interests include conspiracy theories, the Knights Templars and has a fascination for the paranormal and supernatural. Which may explain why he wrote 2020-Wipeout a couple of years before Covid-19 had ever been heard about!